PALM CIRCLE PRESS

SHORT STORY ANTHOLOGY
— 2021 —

*Join the mailing list at **palmcirclepress.net** to receive advanced notice of new releases and for the chance to receive FREE books.*

PALM CIRCLE PRESS

SHORT STORY ANTHOLOGY
— 2021 —

EDITED BY LEE ANDERSON

PALM CIRCLE
PRESS

Printed in the United States of America
ISBN: 978-1-7359325-5-2

Book Design by Oladimeji Alaka

Interior Design by Rachel Greene for elfinpen designs

Published by Palm Circle Press
www.palmcirclepress.net

"The Good Cat" by Vicki Hendricks first published online in Retreats from Oblivion: The Journal of Noircon.

CONTENTS

FOREWORD

LEE ANDERSON

Palm Circle Press was born on October 22nd, 2019, named after the street I grew up on. My goal in starting this publishing house was to release literature too harsh or edgy for the mainstream. My books will be nothing if not daring.

That's why I'm so incredibly proud of this anthology. I'm proudest of how the diversity in these stories abstractly synchs with their similarities. There's an odd alchemy at work. There's a touching love poem written by a 105-year-old woman. There's a story about a woman murdering her husband to escape his abuse. There's even a story about alien abduction.

Every written work in here is exceptionally powerful. They serve as perfect examples for how language can so heavily impact the human soul. We should even cringe to think what this says about the current state of mankind when a literary submission call brings forth such works of pain and loss. Good writing doesn't blink though, not at Palm Circle Press anyway.

Nothing in this anthology blinks either. Enjoy.

SEDAN DE VILLE

LEONARD NASH

Three weeks after I posted my Craigslist and Autotrader ads, lowered the price four times, re-edited my photos, fielded dozens of horseshit texts, emails, and voice messages, and gotten two *Notice of Violation* letters from the property manager about the car leaking fluids onto their precious new asphalt downstairs from my rented condo, a guy calls me, Vladimir something-or-other, a czarist-sounding last name I couldn't make out. Said he'd recently arrived in South Florida from some little town in Russia, a *shtetl*, or something like that. Apparently his crack at the American Dream required a Sedan de Ville with a V-8 engine, rear-wheel drive, and a trunk the size of a shipping container.

"Does your car have a vinyl top?" he said.

"Padded vinyl top, AM/FM stereo, cornering lamps, cruise control, the whole shebang. Everything it came with."

"Leather seats?"

"White leather all the way around. It's like going to the dentist. You can tilt the front seats up, down, back and forth—any direction you like. You could get a root canal on the way home from work."

"My teeth are very good," he said. "When can I see the automobile? I am taking an Uber from where I am staying in Tamarac."

"I'm showing houses all day tomorrow," I said. "How about Friday morning, early? I've got business after lunch." I offered him instructions for using the new virtual security kiosk, but he said if the driver took any pride in his profession, he'd figure it out. Fact is, taking an Uber from Tamarac to Hollywood seemed like an expensive ordeal just to test drive an old Cadillac, and good luck trying to parallel park the monstrosity, but he sounded like a serious buyer. If we didn't make a deal, and so long as he wasn't an asshole, I'd offer him a lift to a bus stop, or even the Tri-Rail station near the water tower on Sheridan Street, maybe try sizing him up as a homebuyer, but no way in hell was I schlepping his ass back to Tamarac.

"I'll need cash, by the way, twenty-dollar bills." I didn't need him showing up with rubles or euros or a fold of American hundreds he'd crafted on some fancy color printer so as to rip off my car.

We agreed to meet at nine-fifteen on Friday. He showed up at eight-forty-five while I was fixing my morning oatmeal. I recognized his voice through the kiosk thing. Must have had the driver drop him off outside the complex. When I fly out of Fort Lauderdale-Hollywood International, I roll my luggage out there, if it's not raining or ninety-five degrees, and wait for my cab by the street, figure I'd save a few bucks. I pressed the entry code, told Vladimir my unit number.

I glanced out the kitchen window over the sink to watch for a fat Russian hoofing it through the parking lot. But he bypassed the elevator, took the stairs to the second floor, and arrived at my door. Turns out he wasn't fat, and he looked younger than he'd sounded on the phone. He was five, maybe six years older than me, with hooded eyes, a flared nose, and a few days' worth of beard and mustache. On my father's side, I'm Russian and Eastern European, not that I've ever been over there or speak a lick of the language, but I'm familiar with the hairy thing, probably go through four or five razor blades a month.

"You want coffee or toast or anything?" I said.

"Some coffee is good." He knelt down to pet my cat. She hissed at him and darted into the living room. "Where is the Cadillac? I did not see it in the parking lot."

"Around the corner, in front of another building." Truth is, I got up early and moved the car to a different guest spot rather than let him see puddled antifreeze and engine oil where I usually parked it. I'm a Realtor, so I'm held to all sorts of ethics and standards and codes of conduct and blah, blah, blah, but I'm not a car dealer. If he wanted to scoot under the Cadillac and sniff around, or take the thing to a mechanic, fine, but I wasn't going to draw him a picture.

"When I get a house," he said, "I will have a Doberman Pinscher."

"Here we can't have dogs over twenty pounds."

"It is like the Soviet Union in these Florida condos," Vladimir said. "I am renting a room from a friend in Tamarac. I met him on the airplane coming over here. I cannot barbecue a steak on the balcony or use the swimming pool after nine o'clock. But fuck them. Sometimes I go downstairs after midnight and swim naked."

I didn't need his life story. I just wanted to unload my old car, then go out and sell some real estate. The Mazda dealership had offered me seven hundred in trade, which was bullshit, even with the various fluid leaks, but I would have saved myself some time and aggravation. Vladimir took his coffee black. I served it to him in a *Café Du Monde* mug, that famous place in New Orleans with the square doughnuts, "beignets" I think they're called. I went there once, but I bought the mug years later at the Salvation Army while shopping for a tuxedo to wear to some fancy banquet thing my girlfriend Monica had dragged me to. I don't know…maybe ex-girlfriend. It's complicated.

So after some chitchat over coffee, I dropped our empty mugs into the sink, grabbed the car keys, the manila envelope with the title from the Florida Division of Motor Vehicles, my Miami Marlins baseball cap, also from the Salvation Army, or maybe Goodwill, and we went downstairs to see the car, two tons of American sheet metal and glorious chrome bumpers basking in the mid-December sunlight.

"Your advertisement said nineteen hundred dollars, yes? That is a lot."

"It has just thirty-seven thousand miles." It sounded like bullshit, but it was true. "I bought the car from an old lady named Esther in Hallandale Beach. Couldn't have been more than four-foot-ten. Said after her husband died, she only took the car to the doctor, the supermarket, CVS, and to the condo across the street to play mahjong. She'd kept it parked under her oceanfront high-rise.

"Automobiles should be driven," Vladimir said. He ran his finger along the gap between the hood and fender. "It is the original paint," he said, a statement not a question. "What is this color?"

The car was a vague metallic-tan, but General Motors called it "taupe." It's like when I needed to fix a lamp, so I took the broken screw-down part to Bed Bath & Beyond. The clerk said it was called a "finial." Monica once told me the wedge in our upper lip is called a "philtrum." All these people with their fancy words...it's not like I'm going on *Jeopardy!*

"Taupe," I said.

"Top?" he said.

"Taupe. Look, just call it 'brown.'"

"No, no," Vladimir said. "I will be an American citizen one day. I want to learn everything."

I was trying to sell my car and this guy wanted a civics lesson.

Leaving for the test drive, he nearly hit the outbound security gate. We drove through the neighborhood south of my condo, past the high school on Harding Street, then north on Federal Highway. He gunned the engine through the yellow light at Sheridan Street. On Dania Beach Boulevard, we went by the jai-alai fronton, turned right on Fifth Avenue, past the abandoned King's Head Pub, and south again toward my place. He observed how there were two Publix supermarkets, two Walgreens, and three Dollar Trees within a mile radius of my condo. "You are a very rich country," he said.

"It's convenient," I said, "but their stuff isn't free."

Back in the parking lot, Vladimir tested the cigarette lighters, all four of them.

"Do you smoke?" I said.

"Cigarettes are not healthy," Vladimir said. He checked under the hood, pulled the dipstick, wiped it with a paper napkin he pulled from his pocket. He measured the tread of each tire with a penny. "I can pay you one thousand dollars. It is leaking antifreeze and oil and perhaps power steering fluid. Also, I wanted a white Cadillac. That has always been part of my dream."

If my car had been white, he would have said he dreamed of owning a red Cadillac. Or *taupe*, for that matter. I should have suggested he go out there and keep looking, because for every old lady pushing a walker with a pair of tennis balls on the legs — to keep them from scraping the linoleum in her kitchen — there's a low-mileage Cadillac or Lincoln Continental or Lexus or Buick being driven by a live-in nurse's aide from Haiti or Nicaragua or Guatemala. Week after week, these cars are offered for sale by family members who spent a week in Florida disposing of Grandma's old lady furniture and dusty *tzotchkes* from a curio cabinet illuminated

6

by a fish tank light bulb. And they hire a Realtor to sell the apartment or musty old house with the leaking roof. Like I said, that was what I did—lease and sell real estate—hence my purchase of the Cadillac in the first place. Monica was never impressed with the humongous car, she with the fancy Mercedes C-Class convertible she'd just paid cash for. Of course, a Miata might've seemed like an odd choice for a Realtor, but frankly, I was done toting people around. I'm a salesman. My job is to show up.

"I cannot accept one thousand dollars for my vehicle." An hour with this guy, and already I felt my syntax changing, a subtle slip toward night school ESOL.

We went back and forth on the price and settled at twelve hundred. The rebuilt AC compressor last summer had cost me half of that.

I shook his rock-hard hand, probably calloused from some sort of construction work, and reached into my pants pocket for the title.

"We must go to the bank," Vladimir said.

"Fine," I said, "we'll find a nearby branch," and given some bad experiences I've had giving signed titles to buyers who never registered the cars in their own name, I decided I'd also accompany him to the tag agency on Park Road, but we'd need to make it quick. At three-thirty I had an appointment to show a couple from Connecticut a vacant townhouse in Emerald Hills, said they needed something they could close in thirty days. Got to love desperate home buyers.

Vladimir waited by the car while I went upstairs, grabbed my wallet, fed the cat, took a leak. I searched his bank on my GPS app. The only branch in Broward County was in Margate—not far from motherfucking Tamarac. But at least I was unloading the car.

*

Heading up I-95—I was driving the two of us in the Cadillac—he asked me about insurance and whether it was required in Florida. "Of course," I said. "The DMV needs proof of coverage before they'll issue you a tag. You haven't arranged for that yet?"

7

"But there is a license plate already."

"That's mine," I said. "When we're done, I have to mail it to Tallahassee."

"Tallahassee is the capital of Florida," Vladimir said. "Do you recommend your insurance agent?"

I could have suggested my State Farm guy, whose building we'd passed during the test drive, but he was a putz, and besides, we were already several miles north of the airport. Vladimir mentioned an insurance agency he'd seen in Lauderhill next to a barber shop.

So that was our first stop, about four hundred bucks for some basic six-month policy. "This ain't even in English," the agent said, holding Vladimir's Russian driver's license. She was a twenty-something African American woman with long, fake purple fingernails embedded with funky little stars. I wondered how she managed her bathroom business.

Vladimir pulled out his Russian passport, but that didn't help.

"Don't strip mall insurance agencies have ways around Russian driver's licenses?" I said.

"Sorry, sir," the woman said to me, ignoring Vladimir like a doctor speaking to a family about a patient's devastating diagnosis, "but the man needs a Florida driver's license—or New Jersey, or Chicago, or wherever. Something in English."

She gave us directions to the DMV up in Margate, in yet another strip mall. We drove over there, and Vladimir parked himself on a bench out front to study the driver's handbook. By this time, I trusted the guy enough to leave him the keys so he could take the road test. Or maybe I just didn't care anymore. "Call me when you're done," I said.

I wandered the length of the strip mall—the DMV was all the way at the west corner. I went in and out of stores, looking for nothing in particular, and thinking how I absolutely should have dumped the car on the Mazda dealership. Or maybe not leased the Miata in the first place. The whole thing had been Monica's idea. She's a hedge fund portfolio manager down in Miami. What was I even doing with such a person?

In Winn-Dixie, I pushed around a cart, putting stuff in—Rice-A-Roni, sardines, Cremora, store-brand corn flakes, a grapefruit, two jars of pickles, a bag of kitty litter, then I backtracked through the store, placing everything back exactly where I'd found it. I'd rather shop closer to home. I paid for a large banana and a cold twenty-ounce bottle of Diet Pepsi in the ten items or fewer lane. I ate the banana and drank my soda on a bench like Vladimir's. The ownership group of that strip mall knew their clientele. Another ex, the one before Monica, moved back to Denver last summer, said she didn't feel motivated in South Florida. Some places had hiking trails, jazz clubs, and world-class museums. Broward County has benches everywhere, and the supermarkets provide blood pressure machines and motorized grocery carts for zipping up and down the aisles with arthritic knees and bad hips.

At Office Depot, I farted around in the computer aisle, spoke with a salesman about a laptop I had no intention of buying. At TJ Maxx, I tried on a polyester blend suit. It fit okay, but I didn't need it. Besides my thrift store tuxedo, I had a wool Saks Fifth Avenue suit with satin-lined trousers I'd found at a garage sale for twenty bucks, hanging from a guy's avocado tree. At Marshall's I bought some woven boxer shorts, factory seconds, but I couldn't tell the difference through the package. I was crossing the street toward another strip mall, in the direction of a Starbucks, when Vladimir called.

"Such an easy exam," he said outside the DMV. "I memorized that silly pamphlet in twenty minutes. In the United States, they give driver's licenses to retarded people, yes?"

"I don't know," I said.

He looked at his new license, held it in the sunlight. "The more I get older, I look like my father, he should rest in peace. He worked in an asbestos factory. It is time for lunch."

"I had something at the supermarket," I said.

"That is no good. I will buy you a fine lunch, and then we will see the insurance lady with the crazy fingernails. Let us go to Ikea," Vladimir said. "They have Swedish meatballs."

"There's a Chinese place across the street. I've got real estate clients later today, and we need to finish up with the car already."

"You have everything in America," Vladimir said, across from me in the red vinyl booth, before a steaming bowl of wonton soup and a plate piled with scoops from the buffet. "Every city is like Disneyland, and you do not appreciate it."

I was having soup too, a mix of egg-drop and wonton, and a plate of cashew chicken and beef chow mein. I thought of Warren Zevon's "Werewolves of London."

"Except for a few years I spent substitute teaching, I've never really been poor," I said, feeling a little guilty about it, "but I've seen poverty."

"You are a good man," Vladimir said. "You are educated, and you are wise, but many Americans are not too smart. That idiot president you elected the other time ... America cannot afford such foolishness.

"Which one?" I said.

"Your Cadillac is old," Vladimir continued, "but for me it represents new opportunities. One day soon, I will drive a fine luxury automobile, and my English will be good, and I will have a three-story house with my own swimming pool and grafted fruit trees and a pocket billiards table and a fireplace and a circular driveway and Thermador appliances."

"You get all this from *Architectural Digest*?"

"And I will have my Doberman Pinscher, and I will have a beautiful wife—maybe American, maybe Russian, maybe a black woman with long fingernails—it is all okay. Today I received my American driver's license, and soon I will be a successful building contractor. Perhaps I will stay in Florida, or maybe I will go to California. I could be the governor there, yes?"

"I suppose," I said, "if that's what you want."

At the register, Vladimir opened his wallet, pulled out some singles, said he'd spent the rest of his cash at the DMV. So far, I'd bought a banana, a Diet Pepsi, a package of underwear, and a lunch buffet for myself, and maybe the next governor of California, and I was still stuck with the goddamn Cadillac.

"Your food is very good," Vladimir said to the man at the cash register as he pawed the fake branches of the countertop Christmas tree beside a goldfish bowl stocked with after-dinner mints.

*

Back at the insurance agency, Vladimir's new Florida driver's license was a big hit with the fingernail lady. "Very handsome," she said. "How do you pronounce your last name? It's like you ain't got enough vowels."

Vladimir smiled and filled out his check.

"My manager won't approve a temporary check," she said. "To issue a binder, we need a regular check with your permanent address printed on it."

"What about cash?" Vladimir said.

"Cash is cool," she said, tapping a purple fingernail on her desktop.

*

If he'd signed up with Wells Fargo, we could have walked across the parking lot to the outparcel near Taco Bell. Instead we drove over to Vladimir's bank on Nob Hill Road. I stood beside him as he withdrew $1,710 in cash. He asked for seventeen $100 bills and five $2 bills. I'd asked for twenties, but I could see the money coming straight from the teller's hands, and at this point, he could have paid me in nickels. Shekels for that matter. I just wanted to get this over with. "Here," he said, "a down payment," and handed me a two dollar bill.

"They still make these?" I said, looking at the image of Thomas Jefferson. It was printed in 1995, so maybe they didn't. The backside featured an engraving of the signing of the Declaration of Independence.

"Americans have much to learn about America. This is valid U.S. currency, legal tender, and you forget it exists. I used some one dollar coins with your eighth president, Mr. Martin Van Buren, at a pharmacy where I'm buying a *New York Times*. The cashier says I should pay with regular money. This is why the driver's examination is designed for idiots."

So on the way back to the insurance office, after he'd prattled through the list of one dollar coins, which skipped the former presidents still living, we were waiting for a red light when the Cadillac overheated, steam billowing from under the hood like an angry pot of boiling spaghetti.

"This presents a problem," Vladimir said.

"No shit," I said as I pulled into a Shell station. After I called AAA, I texted my prospects for the townhouse. *Thanks anyway,* they responded, but they'd found a buy-owner deal, a FSBO as we say in the trade, and were presenting a cash offer with no appraisal or inspection contingencies.

"I've seen worse," the AAA driver said about forty-five minutes later. "Unless you want a tow down to Hollywood, I know a water pump and radiator guy over in Oakland Park."

*

At six-thirty that evening, we stood at the customer service counter at J's Radiator and Air Conditioning with an invoice for $955.37. I looked at it, then at Vladimir. "Holy shit," I said.

"At this moment, your license plate remains on the automobile."

I handed my credit card to the mechanic's wife, her rolls of fat bunched into her hot pink T-shirt with a silkscreen image of Floyd the Barber from the old Andy Griffith Show. Her basset hound slept on the floor beside a fire extinguisher, an oscillating fan, and stacks of Chilton's repair manuals.

"Nine hundred and fifty-five dollars!" I said in the dark gravel lot as we climbed back into the Cadillac.

Under the map light, I studied the itemized invoice, about three payments on the Miata, and hundreds more than my recent commission for leasing a shitty one-bedroom condo across the street from the Golden Isles Post Office. I should have traded the car to the Mazda dealer, or sold it to the scrap yard that had been texting me, or just pushed it into a canal.

"So are you still buying my car?"

"I do not understand that woman's blouse," Vladimir said.

12

"Pink Floyd," I said. "It's a joke."

"I will make you supper," Vladimir said. "And on Monday morning, you come back, and we will go see the fingernail lady. I like her."

"She's a peach," I said. I clicked off the map light, folded the yellow paper into my shirt pocket, against my two dollar bill, started the car, and headed west into the crawl of going-home traffic on Commercial Boulevard, then north on Rock Island Road. Toward Vladimir's place. In Tamarac.

OPHELIA AT 30

KELLY JEAN FITZSIMMONS

Crying my eyes out on the subway without caring who watched was one of the ways I'd learned to negotiate the unrelenting whirr of New York City. I'd honed this skill the year I caught the bouquet at my best friend's wedding in Florida, only to have my boyfriend dump me when we got back home. For the majority of my day, I slapped on a smile and pretended I wasn't devastated to be thirty and single, again, while my best friend was on her honeymoon. Each morning on my way to work, however, I allowed myself the luxury of sobbing uncontrollably on the subway. Bundled up next to my fellow straphangers, tears rolled down my cheeks as freely as the beads of sweat trickling down my back beneath my winter layers. This daily mass transit weep-fest continued for weeks. Until one morning Hamlet got on the A train.

I didn't want Hamlet, aka Shawn Kosminsky, to see me cry. I cared that, with my smeared make-up and snotty nose, he'd think I was still the same weepy hot mess as when we were on tour together. I didn't want him to see that I'd never become a successful actress, or any kind of actress. Why was he here now? Was this a cosmic joke? If Ophelia hadn't descended into her watery grave, would she have been doomed to commute to a boring day job with the Melancholy Dane in the next seat?

I avoided his gaze, but it was too late. Eyes brightening with recognition, he moved toward me. The *Hamlet* tour was my first year out of college, my freshmen year of grownup life, and the last time we'd seen each other.

When Shawn's dopey brown eyes caught my bloodshot ones, he greeted me with Hamlet's words. Ophelia's reply automatically tumbled forth from my lips. Seven years ago, I'd spent weeks drilling those lines into my brain. Once they'd taken hold, they never let go:

"The fair Ophelia! Nymph, in thy orisons be all my sins remember'd."

"Good my lord, how does your honour for this many a day?"

"I humbly thank you; well, well, well."

"My lord, I have remembrances of yours, that I have longed long to re-deliver; I pray you, now receive them."

*

"Longed, *long*," Jack said, correcting me as he looked up from my *Hamlet* script. The Florida sun leaked through the half-closed blinds of his bedroom window, falling in sunny slashes across his thin, freckled chest. It was warm and bright outside, even though it was the last day of December. Half-naked in his bed at the "Boys' House"—the nickname for the place Jack shared with three other guys—he was helping me run my lines. The Boys' House was just as I'd left it—littered with pizza boxes and empty soda cans, dirty dishes crusting slowly in the sink, and the constant background noise of video games. I'd broken up with Jack more than once during college, but this time I'd simply left him behind in Florida after graduation. Back from Shakespeare & Company, while on hiatus from *Hamlet* rehearsals for the holidays, I'd slipped under Jack's red hand-stitched Superman comforter and back into his bed, as if six months were no big deal. Because for me, it wasn't.

"No, that's right," I replied. "Ophelia's nervous about betraying Hamlet, so she's like flustered. Peter says she's correcting herself. That I have longed, *long* to re-deliver."

"Yeah, I get it. He's a freakin' brilliant director. But you said longed, *longed*. Not longed, *long*," Jack said. He reached for his coffee on the nightstand, which was actually a tall stack of white banker boxes housing his comic book collection.

Bringing the Kermit the Frog mug I'd given him for Christmas last year to his mouth, his tongue darted out to lick the edge. Jack always licked the edge of his coffee mug before each and every sip. After years of on-again, off-again dating, there were days I wanted to scream at him, "Just drink it!"

"Do you want to stop?" I asked.

"No. I said I'd help," he answered, mumbling between licks and sips. "I just hate thinking of you going back. To that place."

Snatching the Kermit mug away, I kissed Jack quickly before he had a chance to put his tongue back in his mouth.

"I'm here now," I said, "and…my lord, I have remembrances of yours, that I have longed long to re-deliver." Straddling him, I whispered in his ear, "I pray you, now receive them."

Faces pressed close together, Jack ran one hand down my bare back, while the other fumbled for the script. As we kissed, his soft brown eyes peeked open from behind the gold rims of his round glasses to find Hamlet's next line.

"No. Not I," he read. "I never gave you aught."

"My honour'd lord, you know right well you did," I replied, kissing lightly down his chest.

After we finished the scene, and each other, Jack stared at me intensely, not quite sure I was really there. Reaching out, he stroked the back of his hand softly down the side of my jaw, which, as usual, I was clenching. Exhaling, I relaxed my jaw and stared up at the watercolor painting hanging above Jack's bed. It was of a young boy with a sweet Hummel figurine face, standing in a lake. The water came up to his knees, and he held a large half-submerged fishing net. The painting had been hanging in Jack's room since he was a child.

"I've missed the poor little boy with the drowned basketball hoop," I said, laughing at my old joke. Knowing it irritated Jack, I'd always insisted the painting looked like the little boy was standing next to a submerged basketball hoop.

"It's not a drowned basketball hoop!" Jack mock-sputtered, tickling me as I stubbornly protested the little boy was a tiny flood victim. I loved driving Jack crazy, and he loved me.

Pulling on his ratty green terry cloth robe, Jack swaggered toward the kitchen, a geeky Hugh Heffner, to get us some food. When he was gone, I checked my Hotmail account on his computer. Opening my inbox, I found a flirty email from an older actor I'd been involved with at Shakespeare & Company that summer, the leading man in the outdoor main stage show. Being part of the ensemble, I would watch from the mosquito-filled woods as he made his grand entrance, swinging out of a tall tree on a rope. He'd show up unexpectedly at my company house in his black sports car, with his sloppy golden retriever hanging out the window. We'd drive to some lush forgotten field and take long walks while his dog ran free ahead of us. He was going through a divorce, and we talked about that, and Shakespeare, and what it was like to be a professional actor in New York City—where I was thinking about moving someday soon.

His email asked if I was doing anything fun tonight, for New Year's Eve. Writing back, I told him I planned to celebrate by camping out on the beach with friends, so we could watch the first sunrise of 2000. I omitted the fact I'd just been naked in bed with one of those friends. Then, I wrote something I knew he'd love to read. Words I would later regret because they weren't true.

Happy New Year! I'll be thinking of you when the sun rises.

After a while, Jack wandered back in, fixated on the cover of a Fantastic Four comic book, *sans* food.

"You know," he said, "I always thought the Silver Surfer was the saddest of all comic heroes. Flying around in the vast vacuum of space, all alone..."

"Jack," I snapped. "The food?"

"Sorry," he said. "Emma's in the kitchen and I... I'll go back out and grab something in a minute."

"Why's she here? I thought he didn't want anything to do with her?"

My life had unwillingly intermingled with Emma Ryan's for years. All through college we competed over acting roles, over men, then, when she was dating Jack's best friend and roommate, over being the Alpha girlfriend at the Boys' House. We both ended up going to Shakespeare & Company after graduation, both stayed on to direct shows in their Fall Festival. Now, also on break from working on a smaller festival the company had in the spring, Emma was back in Florida too.

"You didn't tell her about tonight, did you?" I asked. Emma glommed on to things, and I didn't want her to come with us to the beach. Jack and I were doubling with my best friend and her boyfriend. We didn't need a fifth wheel.

"No," Jack replied, "but I don't think she has any—"

"No way," I said, cutting him off. "Stay here. I'll go."

When I walked into the kitchen, Emma was there by herself, doing the dishes. She was the kind of girlfriend who baked and liked a clean sink. I was the kind of girlfriend who scarfed Emma's brownies and refused to touch the boys' mess. Her round face was pallid, and her eyes were red. I felt so sorry for her then, pathetically hanging around her ex-boyfriend's house because she didn't know where else to go.

"Hey," I said.

"Hi," she replied, scrubbing a large plastic colander clogged with dried bits of pasta and congealed pesto sauce. The boys made a lot of pesto, but with canola oil, so I refused to eat it. Emma indicated the dirty colander with a bemused *those boys* smile. Rolling my eyes in response, I went over to the refrigerator.

"How's rehearsal?" she asked.

"Good-ish," I replied, then added, "Tough. Peter's torturing me."

"He sees something in you," Emma said. Her pale lips tightly pursed as she scrubbed.

I know, I silently gloated.

Peter had created the Fall Festival of Shakespeare, an education program where young directors, like Emma and I, immersed hundreds of high school students in an intense production of a Shakespeare play. Then all the schools came together to perform their shows for the public on Shakespeare & Company's main stage in one long, passionate, exhausting, hormone-infused weekend. Peter was our leader, our mentor. He taught us to breathe our souls into the air. Emma and I had volleyed for Peter's attention that fall. We'd both auditioned to be Ophelia in the spring. I'd landed the role. We stood in stretched silence as I foraged in the nearly barren fridge for something edible.

"Weird being here, huh?" I said finally.

"What about you and Jack? Is that weird?" she asked, looking up from the lost-cause colander.

"No," I answered, lying. "We're just enjoying things while we can."

Emma knew about my summer fling. *Flings,* truth be told. Now here I was, back with Jack, as if none of that had happened. We'd both come home again, and I didn't need her puffy judgment eyes to remind me you can't do that. Closing the fridge, I left before she could ask about our New Year's Eve plans. Jack and I hid in his room for the rest of the afternoon. Cuddling under the covers, we whispered about how annoying it was that Emma wouldn't leave.

*

And Emma and I slept together. Once.

Jack's words sat static on the glowing computer screen, but I kept staring at them, willing the letters to magically rearrange themselves to read something, anything else.

I'd been back at Shakespeare & Company for a little over a month when Jack left me an anxious voicemail during *Hamlet* rehearsal. "Have you checked your email?" he'd asked. It was Jack who had sent me to the company's office to check my Hotmail while on a dinner break from rehearsal. Opening his message, I was blindsided by a completely unfiltered stream-of-consciousness rant of every awful thing I'd ever done to him since we'd met sophomore year.

The dense block of angry text, with its ALL CAPS and urgent exclamation points (!!!!) screamed at me before I could even take in the raw fury of his words. The worst part was every single vicious thing Jack wrote about me was true. I'd taken his love for granted, toyed with his affections, broken up with him repeatedly, once over his birthday even—after going to Shakespeare & Company the first time, for an acting intensive, and falling hard for my scene partner. He wrote how happy he'd been when we got back together, and stayed together, only to have me leave him again, and again, for that damn place, to hook up with God-knows-who because I was the one who selfishly didn't want a long-distance relationship.

Scrolling down and down through the tirade, just when I thought I'd reached the end of my crimes against him, I read that Jack had accessed my email account and read through the flirty messages I'd exchanged with my other leading man. This included the one I'd sent New Year's Eve, moments after Jack and I had been in bed together. How had Jack hacked my Hotmail? Simple. I'd given him my password so he could check something for me while I was at my parents' house. I didn't think twice about doing this because it was Jack, the most genuine guy I'd ever known.

After I had left, Jack wrestled with temptation for weeks before giving in and reading my emails. Hating himself for violating my trust, and hurt I'd betrayed him, again, his ambush hate message wasn't written entirely out of malice but self-preservation. It was a stake through the heart of our relationship in hopes of finally, permanently, ending things. To be free of the pain that was me. Near the end, Jack bluntly confessed:

And Emma and I slept together. Once. We were never going to tell anyone. And I haven't till now.

Those immobile words sitting on the screen were grief and murder balled up in the hot knot of my stomach. Finally understanding how Jack felt each time I'd cut him with my indiscretions, I doubled over in my chair, tears falling in small splashes on my muddy snow boots. Pushing away from the computer, I got up and pulled open a gap in the yellowing blinds to look out the window of the old two-story New England house that doubled as the company's shared office. The street below was bleakish, covered in muddy clumps of plowed snow. The soft glow of old-fashioned streetlamps outlined the boney reach of the trees' barren branches. It wasn't even 5 p.m., but already too black outside to see the Berkshire Mountains rising in the distance.

I tried to picture the little boy with the drowned basketball hoop hovering over Jack as he sat in his sunny bedroom in Florida (yesterday afternoon, according to the email's timestamp,) angrily clacking out his heartbreak on his keyboard. Just a few weeks ago, I'd snuggled up next to good 'ole Jack as the sun warmed the blue-gray sky, then popped brightly over the horizon. A new millennium of adventure and uncertainty awaited us. It was comforting to spend those first few moments together. Now the warm Florida sun, Jack, and our bodies intertwined under his Superman comforter no longer existed in this Bizarro World. Turning off the computer, the office plunged into darkness.

*

"I did love you once."

"Indeed, my lord, you made me believe so."

Back in rehearsal, we were running the nunnery scene. I tried to focus on the play, but Jack's words kept crawling across the bottom of my brain, tiny news tickers of agony.

And Emma and I slept together. Once.

"You should not have believed me, for virtue cannot so inoculate our old stock but we shall relish of it. I loved you not," Shawn Kosminsky's Hamlet said. All I heard was Jack.

See, even me, the perfect boyfriend, always the goddamn nice guy, gentleman, your whole family loves me, I'm such a better person than other guys, whatever that's a load of crap.

"I was the more deceived," my Ophelia replied.

"Get thee to a nunnery. Why wouldst thou be a breeder of sinners?" Hamlet asked, grabbing my arm. "I am myself indifferent honest, but yet I could accuse me of such things that it were better my mother had not borne me."

I read your emails. You told him you would think of HIM at sunrise. I HATE YOU SO MUCH FOR DOING THIS TO ME!!! You-fucking-bitch. Oh God, I love you so much…

He'd gone crazy and stabbed my heart through an electronic curtain.

"What should such fellows as I do crawling between earth and heaven? We are arrant knaves, all, believe none of us," Hamlet shouted as he threw the prop love letters we used as the remembrances Ophelia longed, *long* to re-deliver in my face.

"Rip them up," Peter interrupted. Directing Shawn's Hamlet, Peter paced back and forth, chomping on nicotine gum with a mischievous glint in his eye.

"Back it up to 'You should not have believed me' and tear them up," he said, "Throw them right in her face, wherever feels right."

We ran the nunnery scene again, and again, with Hamlet ripping up his "love letters" to me in such a spiteful manner that, to this day, if you shred paper in my face, I will cry.

"O, woe is me, to have seen what I have seen, see what I see!" I whimpered, desperate for the scene to be over, for rehearsal to be

24

over. All I wanted was go back to my lonely little room in my company house, crawl under the covers, and forget the world.

"Higher," Peter said, "Listen to how the low O's, *ohhhhh*, woe, flip up to these high-pitched E's in me and seen what I have seen." Pointing towards the ceiling, he sent his E's into the stratosphere. "See what I *seeee*! Hear that? The language indicates her state of mind. Ophelia's keening in grief. Try it again."

Eager to please Peter, I flipped my deep voice up to an uncomfortably high register, pushing the line out in a forced banshee wail. "O, woe is me, to have seen what I have seen, see what I see!"

I wanted to master Shakespeare's high E's and cry so Peter would think I was an amazing actress, but the tears wouldn't come. Only, maybe this time his direction wasn't entirely brilliant. I thought about Ophelia's E's and how my voice sometimes went high and tight when fighting to control my tears. I didn't need a linguistic trick to inform me of the grief Ophelia felt seeing the person she loved go mad. Or the clawing fear that she'd destroyed his kind spirit with her betrayal.

*

Tomorrow is Saint Valentine's day.
All in the morning betime

Our invited dress rehearsal for *Hamlet* was on Feb 13th. I remember this distinctly because I thought it was cool that when I sang "Tomorrow is Saint Valentine's Day" during my madness scene, it really would be. Unfortunately, I couldn't sing to save my life. I could still hear Peter's frustrated note to me, "You have three songs. You think you could find a tune in one of them?" Taking his words to heart, I dutifully plunked out Ophelia's madness songs on the piano in the rehearsal room before every show, trying to train my tone-deaf ears.

Since we were a touring production, the invited dress, which we performed for the other Shakespeare & Company members, served as our opening night. Shortly before our audience arrived, my friend playing Claudius came up to me with two deliveries. The first was a massive bouquet of flowers from Jack, along with a card that read, *Congratulations! And Happy Valentine's day! If this arrives late, I guess Break a leg! Love, Jack.*

Each "i" was dotted with a cute little circle. His message had been written out by the florist when he'd ordered the flowers for Valentine's Day and our opening. The second delivery was Jack's atrocious email. When I didn't respond to it, the radio silence had caused him to snap even further, print it out, and mail the five-page email to me. Love and hate had caught up to each other in-transit and arrived on the same day.

Holding the flowers in one hand, the letter in the other, I shook them both at Claudius, shrieking, "What the hell am I supposed to do with this?"

Already in costume, Claudius simply readjusted his over-sized gaudy crown, trying hard not to laugh at my tantrum.

I entertained the idea of switching out the prop love letters Hamlet shredded in my face for Jack's hate letter, but I couldn't bring myself to do it. During the madness scene, I sang "Tomorrow is Saint Valentine's Day" straight from my gut without hitting a single note. Tomorrow really was Valentine's Day, and really going mad from grief and betrayal, I belted out the words:

> *And I a maid at your window,*
> *To be your Valentine.*
> *Then up he rose, and donn'd his clothes,*
> *And dupp'd the chamber-door;*
> *Let in the maid, that out a maid*
> *Never departed more.*

With everyone in the company, including Emma, watching, I completely lost my shit on stage. Peter had directed me to kiss Claudius as part of my madness, but in my Madness 2.0 frenzy, I nearly tackled that rat bastard to the ground, knocking the crown clean off his head.

> *By Gis, and by Saint Charity,*

'Alack! and, fie for shame!
Young men will do't, if they come to't;
By Cock, they are to blame.

Jack and Emma together, naked, touching, laughing, filled me with rage. What had they whispered to each other about me? Even worse was the thought of all the times Jack and I had been together since he'd had sex with her. Without the aid of any high E's, I dissolved into real, snotty, ugly tears.

"There's rosemary, that's for remembrance; pray, love, remember: and there is pansies. That's for thoughts." When I re-entered, passing out flowers, I gave away the bright blossoms from Jack's poorly-timed bouquet. Their sticky-sweet scent clung to my hands as I flung them around the stage.

"There's rue for you, and here's some for me." Looking past Gertrude, into the audience, I spoke directly to Emma as I handed the Queen Jack's flowers as her *rue*, or *ruta graveolens*, a bitter herb associated with adultery, regret, and everlasting suffering. Never again would I be Jack's one and only girl. Now, I was only his first bitch.

And will he not come again?
And will he not come again?
No, no, he is dead:
Go to thy death-bed:
He never will come again.

Singing softly, and off-key, I numbly drifted offstage. For the rest of the run, I couldn't live up to that performance. Turned out I was only an amazing actor when not acting. Whenever he dropped in on the tour to see the show and give us notes, Peter would say, "Do you remember the invited dress? You had us all in tears. Do the madness scene like that."

I would nod, accepting his feedback, but inside I screamed, "Don't you understand, that would kill me!"

It killed Ophelia, didn't it? Loving too much, losing too much.

*

My heartbreak didn't kill me, but when Hamlet appeared on the A train I remembered how much it felt like the end of the world back then. My current subway tears paled in comparison. At least now I had the cold comfort of knowing I wouldn't always feel this way. That along with the love, the pain faded.

"The fair Ophelia," Shawn Kosminsky smiled as he pushed his way through the subway car, "Nymph, in thy orisons, be all my sins remember'd." We did an awkward *hello* dance, half-hugging. I avoided shaking his hand since my blue mittens were crusted in snot from wiping my runny nose. We had a nice catch-up conversation. Shawn had been living in the city all these years as well and was now doing social work with troubled teens.

Not exactly the scene one might imagine if Ophelia really did run into Hamlet, years later, on their way to work. But Ophelia and Hamlet were dead, destroyed by their passions. If Ophelia had made it to thirty, maybe she would have gotten a chance to find the strength and power behind her madness. *Lord, we know what we are, but know not what we may be.*

I never imagined I would see Jack again, especially when, about a year after the *Hamlet* tour, he married Emma. But not too long after that, they divorced. When Jack moved to New York for a fresh start, I was the one who gave him a place to stay. Then, in our own Shakespearian twist of fate, Jack's cousin married my best friend. Seven years after we'd camped out on the beach to watch the first sunrise of 2000.

Both in the wedding party, Jack and I stood next to the happy couple at the altar. Though we were at the wedding with other people—Jack with a woman he would later marry, and me with a boy who would dump me a few days later—we seemed forever destined to be part of each other's lives. Our youthful passion had been traded-in for quaint conversation at friends' birthday parties and baby showers, but unlike Hamlet and Ophelia, we were still here. Jack and I never talked about his letter, and I never told him he was the only one I was thinking about as we watched the first sunrise.

EULOGY FOR A
COCA-COLA GLASS

JIM MOSS

Dearly beloved liquid consumers, we are gathered here today around the shattered remains of a Coca-Cola glass. We dare not get too close, lest a crystal shard or two puncture our stocking feet. But we did love this Cola glass. For many years, yea, it was part of our family. Its home was in the cupboard, but oftentimes it patiently sat beside the basin of falling water waiting to be rinsed clean in the churning, purifying Palmolive foam. It held our soda, our milk, our apple cider, our vodka concoctions, and so many other liquids. And we held it, firmly, yet gently in our hands — its ergonomic form allowing us to conveniently sip, swallow, and gulp the lubricants our bodies did require. Our lips would caress its rim, while our hand would tilt it upward to spill its delicious contents into our waiting mouths. Many an evening was spent with this Cola glass in hand as we watched the brightly colored images move across our "box of wasteland vast" or as we reclined with a favorite tome and a basket of salsa and chips. Our fingerprints smudged thee. The remains of our juices collected on thy bottom and solidified into sticky paste. Thy condensation created rings on our coffee table. Thy were accidentally bumped off the table a number of times, and although we became agitated and cursed when thy contents were spilled on the carpet or over an important piece of parchment, we also breathed a sigh of relief when thou did not break or chip. But today was thy final fall. Thy end was mercifully swift. Now we carefully pick up thy remains and drop them into a brown paper bag. As for thy soul, we wish for thee eternal life, to sparkle as never before in the presence of God. The gentle dishwashing wings of angels shall clean and polish thee. Thou shall be filled with ambrosia and touched by God's lips. In thy new cupboard, thou shall meet once again the other vessels with which thee were forged who have likewise fallen. Thy cupboards shall never be shut nor grow dark, but be forever lit by the florescent, neon, and chrome glow of God's Heavenly Diner.

Amen.

YOU WILL BE FINE

HOLLY CARIGNAN

You will grow a thick, lifelong bedrock of fear and humiliation, a hardened, crusted, sedimentary record of your experiences. It starts when you are maybe four, at the community pool, on the slide, and the neighbor, a grown man, stands at the bottom with his arms open wide to catch you. Your parents beckon you from the pool, tell you never, ever to do that again. You don't understand but you feel a hot, hot shame on your sunburnt face.

When you are in kindergarten, a policeman comes to your class and warns you about strangers. You and your classmates line up and, one by one, have your descriptions written down lest you do not heed the warnings. The nurse notes a raised, dark mole on your right shoulder. You didn't know it was there and later look at it in the mirror and decide you hate it. When you are in the second grade, a child you don't know is abducted from a neighborhood with which you are unfamiliar. Your mom discusses this matter with the other moms at the bus stop, and they all cluck and tsk and sigh. You picture sinister, thieving men pushing their way up from Hell and through manholes, aching, ravenous, ready to pluck children off the streets. You cease riding your bicycle for a week.

You develop before the other girls in your class. Keith and Danny needle you at every recess, request a viewing of your tits. That next summer, a pretty girl, one grade higher, gathers a group of girls at the community pool to torment you about the hair under your armpits. Your mother does not permit you to wear a bra or shave. Years later, when you are still waiting to outgrow your anger, you hear fourth-hand that this same girl became a stripper, that she got knocked up by one of her customers. This information satisfies you. You are inspired to locate Keith on Facebook, and find that he has grown fat, his face fleshy and pink. You consider messaging him to see if he, too, now wears a bra, but you see no point in it.

When you are twelve, you ride your bicycle to the community pool and a car slows beside you. This car is a dinged-up Volkswagen Rabbit, its driver shaggy and filthy, and you think of the men who come out of manholes. You make the mistake of looking at his eyes, into the tar pool of his molten core. His tongue practically lolls out of his head like he is a stinking, overheated jackal. He speeds away. You continue on to the pool, your pedaling reaching a fevered momentum. You are hypervigilant, scanning front, back, left, right. You are suspicious of sewer grates. When you arrive, your mother is already there relaxing on a lounger. You, sweaty but cold, gasping, stay by her side for the rest of the afternoon. At the end of the day, your mother is irritable as she tries to maneuver your bicycle into the trunk of her car. This time, you will stay off your bicycle for the rest of the summer.

When you are thirteen, your parents corner you in your bedroom to tell you that you are getting fat. You do something about it. When your period stops, your parents reverse course and try to get you to gain weight. Your mother is angry at your willfulness. She is worried about you but won't know how to tell you. Instead, she picks you up one day in the middle of school and take you to the gynecologist. You aren't entirely naïve, but it has never occurred to you that anyone, or anything, could ever possibly go between your legs and inside your body.

The gynecologist is an old man with glasses, his face wrinkled like a raisin, his breath stale. You see a foreign metal device on a tray next to the bed and the old man tells you to put your feet in the stirrups. You feel cold air on your naked bottom. The old man inserts the device, and it feels like he is slowly opening an umbrella, all spokes and cold metal, into your body. It hurts. A lot. You later go to a lab for bloodwork and faint onto the floor, knock your elbow onto a chair on your way down.

Your mother later drops you off at school and you sit in class shaken and white. You turn and glance at the kid behind you, but don't know why exactly you are doing it. He asks what your problem is. You shrug, turn around. You decide to forget, to stuff the day's events into that crowded wasteland in your memory where such things belong. You will not forget, though—the memory will pop out at you from time to time over the years like a macabre jack-in-the-box. A bruise blossoms above your elbow. The next night your mother sees it while you are brushing your teeth before bed. "Where did that come from?" she will ask.

In high school, you decide that you don't give a fuck about life. But, sorry, you really do give an enormous fuck, about everything, including things about which you are not aware. The mist of a depression starts to settle itself on your skin like a sticky insecticide.

In the tenth grade, you ride your bicycle with your friend, Stacy, and you both pass a man parked on the side of the road and working underneath his car. He is on his back, his face obscured by the floor of the car, his fly open and his penis hanging out like a dead, flaccid eel washed ashore.

A block down the road, Stacy, her face ashen, asks if you saw what she saw. You sputter out a "yes." That is the last time you and Stacy will talk about it, but you will wonder for the rest of your life if that man did it deliberately. You will never know. Sometimes a mystery must stay a mystery.

The year you graduate high school, you see *The Silence of the Lambs* in the theater. It fills you with dread when you are later alone in your dark bedroom. You sleep with the light on that night. And the next. And the next. Until your father asks you not to. That summer, before you leave for the University of Florida, a story about a serial killer murdering five people in that college town will make national headlines. This time, you go to bed with a book light on, but the battery conks out, leaving you alone in the dark. Before you leave home for college, you have that horrid mole removed by a dermatologist who later calls to tell you it is not cancerous. For a fleeting moment, you wonder how they will identify your dead body now but remember with relief that there are always dental records. That fall, at school, you ride your bicycle to class and pass a wall onto which the victims' names have been spray-painted. Every day that semester, as you glide by, you say those names aloud, into the wind, like an elegy.

Before you graduate, you attend a reading by a southern author who is the chair of the creative writing department. He describes Florida as "a penis hanging off the belly of America," and this amuses you. Degree in hand, you move twelve-hundred miles up the east coast, away from your family. You consider yourself independent, worldly. You pack your shit, head north, and wave goodbye to America's penis. Or so you think. You find an apartment, a job, a cat, and you are excited because you figure you will find yourself, too. The cat, fluffy and orange, whom you will name "Pumpkin," winds his way out of the bushes on your running route. He is covered in burrs and thorns, but you pet him anyway. The neighbor comes outside and begs you to take the cat off his hands. You will love that cat with every atom, every proton, neutron, and electron of your being.

One day, two years later, you find a note written on a ragged scrap of paper and stuck under your car's windshield wipers. It says, in a shaky pen, "We are from different worlds, but we are the same." You accuse a man who has been pursuing you for a date of leaving that note on your car. He denies it, and for reasons you don't understand, you believe him. You will never find out who left it there, but you will one day have your suspicions.

Not long after you find the note, you go hiking with some friends, and you all go off the main path. You find the horn of an old Victrola laying in the middle of the forest, just sitting there with nothing else around it. The horn is strangely bright and brassy in that wet forest. You and your friends marvel at this random discovery and circle it like you are in an *X-Files* episode and have discovered a flying saucer.

Your back is tight and throbbing after that hike and you go immediately afterward to buy a real bed. This bed will replace your old futon and you consider this an extravagance, because it is. You put it on your credit card. That night, you spend two hours dismantling the futon and dragging it, piece by piece, out your apartment's sliding door and to the dumpster. You will wonder days later whether you had locked that sliding door before you and Pumpkin fell asleep on your makeshift bed on the floor.

That next morning, before dawn, on March 17th, 2000, you awaken to a stranger, a man shrouded in the blue light of your clock radio. He yanks you up by your hair and tells you that if you scream, he will fucking kill you. You believe him. You know immediately what is about to happen. He gives you simple instructions: turn here, do this, touch that, and you think of these directions as steps in a how-to manual. It is all mechanical and you will do what you must.

You remember, suddenly, that Victrola horn, its random appearance in your life. How, you wonder, did it wind up in the middle of the forest? You question whether it was an omen, a sign of events to come, but you can't come up with a logical connection between a rape and a Victrola. In your mind, you try to draw out complicated diagrams of the connection, make what seems like brilliant mental leaps only to find yourself feeling hopelessly confounded. The man starts a casual conversation with you, asks you your name, your cat's name, what kind of job you have. You lie. You sense a sad loneliness in this man, a pulsing desperation, and you almost feel sorry for him.

The man makes you get in the shower, tells you to count to one hundred. He calls out an apology, his voice trailing—you know he is finally leaving. You count, and you hate each number as it drops out of your mouth. You shut off the spigot, tiptoe wet and scared and weary into your room. He is gone, your sliding door open—the one you may or not have locked. Pumpkin is in a low, tight crouch behind the television. You call the police. And the Victrola? You figure that sometimes a mystery must stay a mystery.

There are squad cars, a swarm of officers, and two detectives. One detective looks like Morgan Freeman, and the other barks his impatience at you because you cannot tell him what surfaces, besides your body, the man may have touched. You request that this detective kindly, please stop, stop, just stop. Your sentence ends in a trailing, bloodless ellipsis. You are dying infinite deaths right here in front of these men, these strangers. Morgan Freeman tells him to cut the shit.

They cover your walls, bathroom doorway, and sliding door with fingerprint powder, bag up your clothes, your bedding, tell you to go to the hospital to have evidence collected off your body. Your body is a crime scene. Pumpkin twines his way around Morgan Freeman's legs. He pats Pumpkin's head.

Over the weeks and months to follow, you meet with Morgan Freeman at the police station to go over your story again and again and again. After each session, Detective Freeman escorts you out the back door and stands on the balcony, his hands resting on the rail, his foot propped on a bottom rung, watching you make your way down the stairs and across the lot to your car. You turn and wave before unlocking the door. You will always remember his kindness.

Several weeks after the assault, it comes to you suddenly, in a synaptic jolt: you know exactly where that note came from. You call Detective Freeman, and he asks you if you still have it. You promise to look for it and tear through your apartment. You do not remember throwing it away, figure it is lurking somewhere. It makes you crazy. You know it is somewhere, somewhere just out of reach. You think about giving up, tell Detective Freeman you can't find it, but you know exactly who left it. You are sure. We may never know, he tells you, a tinge of sorrow in his voice. You continue to look anyway.

You max out two credit cards hiring people to move your belongings into a third-floor apartment with a buzzer. Over the next year, you read about three more rapes in your former apartment complex. The police set up a female decoy in the neighborhood and find a man following her with his zipper undone and his junk hanging out. *Always with the goddamned open flies,* you think to yourself. You are unable to identify his picture, but the DNA speaks for itself.

You attend the man's arraignment. He comes out in shackles. You hear them rattling with his shuffling steps. He looks like he just woke up from a lifelong bender. He is unshaven, his hair long and dark and bushy. He is still entirely unfamiliar, which startles you. But now you know his name. You see a middle-aged couple waving at this man and know, without needing to be told, they are his parents. Fancy that, you think, rapists have names and parents.

After he is arraigned, you go into the bathroom where you nearly collide with the man's mother, who is exiting. You apologize. You drive home and think of all the inane apologies you have made in your life and suddenly understand that it is not you who must apologize. It occurs to you that even the rapist himself knew this. You, too, from then on out, will always know this.

The man cuts a deal with the prosecutor and is sentenced to twenty-four years in prison. You will live your life, with or without purpose. It will be yours to choose. You go back to that forest to look for the Victrola but are unable to find it. You will never find that note or know who put it on your car. You have grown tired of mysteries. You send Morgan Freeman a thank you card. Pumpkin remains your truest love.

For a while, like clockwork, every March 17th, you dream about the rapist. In some of those dreams, you are expecting him, sitting up in your bed and waiting. Oddly, it is not a feeling of dread you have in these dreams, but resigned expectation. He is a part of your bedrock, whether you like it or not. The dreams, though, they eventually stop. In the last dream, he is unable to get through that sliding door. He pulls, tugs, yanks, pounds his fists on this glass, but he cannot get in. His hands bleed. He crumples into a heap. As dawn approaches, he vaporizes like a vampire in a shaft of light.

The rape becomes like an ancient star whose ragged light has traveled through great distances of time and space to reach you so faded that you barely recognize it. You feel no fear now, and you find this odd. It is almost like you have stared into the blinding sun and come out with a greater clarity. You cannot fear death when you have already seen its gaping face.

Ten years after the rape, you jog past a motorcyclist waiting at a stop light. He looks you square in the face and makes an obscene gesture with his tongue. You envision him skidding over an oil slick and laugh. You stop, lift your middle finger at this man, then continue jogging into the deepening dusk.

LOVE POEM

GLADYS DUBOVSKY

I

Shall I say
that my love is as swift
as a bird in its flight?
That my love is as strong
as the wind in its might?

That my love is as fierce
as the wild sun is bright?
That my love is as great
as wrong is from right?

That my love will last
as long as does Time?
My darling, these
are mere words that rhyme.

II

How can the glory of sun
in its heat
be told in that
which is rhythm and beat?

How can the beauty
of birds on the wing
be enclosed in a pen,
of their glamor to sing?

How can I dare
the strength of the wind,
explain it on paper,

lest its might be not dimmed?

III

My love is all this,
yea, much more, by far.
Yet ne'er can I tell you
for fear I would mar
its perfection.

You never will know
how much I love you.
For all I can say
is that I love you.

SNAPSHOTS

DEBBIE SHANNON

When Hootie first saw Brenda in Nick's Bar, she was showing her friends her green tongue from all the Grasshoppers she'd drank. Brenda came in most days after working the lunch shift at the Kountry Kitchen. He watched her sit at the end of the bar counting her tips. Tammy the bartender was her friend and neighbor. They lived next door to one another at the Happy Trails trailer park about a mile down the road.

Tammy had bleach-blonde hair that was usually controlled by a big blue butterfly clip. Wisps of hair escaped the clip and hovered around her face. She swatted at them as though they were flies as she poured drinks. She seemed to come in from the rain no matter what the weather. She wore ripped jeans and a tank top that may have been white. Her sagging breasts were free to move around under the top, nipples facing different customers at the bar. She told dirty jokes and bedded men. And she looked out for Brenda.

Hootie was a carpenter who came to Florida from New Jersey after his divorce. He worked the construction business with his cousin Phil. One day after work, he and Phil stopped in for a beer. They had been regulars ever since. There was something about Nick's Bar that Hootie liked from the start. It wasn't hoity-toity. The bar was dark and smelled of wet corks and hound dog. There were neon Rolling Rock beer signs in the windows and fluorescent lights above the two stained pool tables. Christmas lights surrounded the mirror in back of the bar year-round. An eight-foot NASCAR poster of Jeff Gordon on the paneled wall dangled by two red thumbtacks. The jukebox blared Southern rock.

Hootie sat at the bar watching two guys play pool. The shirtless man with the shaved head had a swastika on his left shoulder. The other guy had long stringy hair and tattooed dragons on his forearms. He wore a black T-shirt that read: "Don't Fuck With Me."

Mr. "Don't Fuck With Me" put his beer bottle on the edge of the pool table and leaned over to take his shot. A cigarette clung to the edge of his bottom lip. Pool balls scattered noisily. The cue ball threatened to jump the railing and flee the scene but bounced back into the center of the table. Cigarette ash plunked onto the green felt. As "Simple Man" by Lynyrd Skynyrd rang out from the jukebox like an anthem, the two guys air-guitared their pool cues.

Hootie glanced toward the end of the bar at Brenda and smiled. He walked to the end of the bar and straddled the stool next to her.

"Hello."

"Hello, yourself," she said. She smiled, swirling the straw in her drink.

Hootie leaned toward her. He smelled rose water. Her bottle-red hair curled around her shoulders. Her eyes were grey, like the sea after a storm. She wore black leggings and a big T-shirt with a cat playing with yarn on the front. The back of the shirt showed the cat walking away, tail lifted. She wore several thin multi-colored bangle bracelets that rattled together whenever she moved. The sound reminded Hootie of the cat he'd had when he was a boy. His mother put a bell on the collar so Fluffy could always be found. Did Brenda want to be found?

They talked and laughed. They shared childhood stories. They shared their dreams.

"The reason you two get along is because you're both Yankees," Tammy said.

Before long, Hootie visited Brenda at the Kountry Kitchen. He'd sit at the counter, order pie and coffee, and watch her wait tables. They'd steal bits of hushed conversation during his coffee refills. Brenda's boss glared.

One evening, Brenda invited him to dinner at her house. Hootie pulled his truck into the driveway and knocked on the screen door.

"It's open," Brenda said from somewhere inside the house. He heard pots bang.

He walked in and looked around the screened patio. Against the inside wall were two green plastic chairs and an end table with a spider plant and a red beanbag ashtray. A clothesline ran the length of the patio. Three wooden clothespins sat on the line like birds. An artificial Christmas tree stood in the back corner. It was August. The tree was littered with plastic Disney ornaments. Dumbo perched on the top holding a star.

Hootie climbed three metal steps and entered the trailer. The interior of the trailer wasn't too different from the bar. An olive-green shag carpet led the eye across the living room to the dark-paneled walls. Christmas lights adorned a framed mirror which hung in the center of the wall. Brenda rushed into the room wearing an apron.

"You want a drink? Is beer okay?" She ran her fingers through her hair.

"Sure. You need help?"

"Nope. Make yourself comfortable." With that she was gone. Pots crashed.

He glanced at the small bookcase filled with unopened Disney videos. Above the bookcase, framed family photos filled the wall.

"These pictures are great." Hootie sank into a powder-blue sofa. He spotted a puffy feather and lace covered photo album underneath the glass coffee table. He picked it up and gently opened the cover.

The first snapshot he saw was of a young Brenda on a tractor. Captions were written in ink on the bottom border of each picture. Brenda, eight-years-old. The young smiling girl in the snapshot waved at the camera. Her long blonde hair blew into the wind like a golden weathervane. Her life was before her, and it held such promise.

The next snapshot: Brenda in Dad's apple tree. The same innocent child swinging from a tree branch, cheeks rosy, apple in her hand. Other snapshots showed a happy Brenda with her two older sisters.

Hootie sat back in the sofa and turned the page. Brenda at Randale High School. A different girl. Older Brenda wore a large sweater and tight jeans, surrounded by girlfriends. Her beautiful golden hair was smothered in dark dye and yanked into a ponytail, a cigarette pinched between fingers in the hand at her side, half-hidden from the camera. The dark lipstick in the black and white snapshot made the girls' mouths appear black. They posed in front of a bowling alley.

Another snapshot of Brenda and the girls in Tim's car. Tim, Hootie assumed, was the older driver. He turned the page. Tim and Brenda. Hootie studied the young couple. Tim had his arm wrenched

51

around Brenda's shoulder, causing her neck to bend at a wrong angle. Her smile looked forced.

He turned the page. Our wedding day. Tim and Brenda. *She's just a kid,* Hootie thought.

"Oh, you found my photo album." Brenda fluttered into the room, handing Hootie a beer. She sat beside him. "I was seventeen and Tim was twenty-four. I told my parents I was going to marry him with or without their consent."

"How long were you married?"

"Two years. Tim had an affair with some floozy at work the first year. Started hitting me the second. I moved back home and got a divorce."

"Why did you marry him? You were so young."

"I wanted to get out of the house. And I didn't want to be a virgin any longer."

"You know, you don't actually have to get married to lose your virginity."

"I wasn't that kind of girl."

Hootie turned the page. Brenda and her friends at another bowling alley wearing pink league shirts. Her flipped up hair was now red. She wore light pink lipstick and sky-blue eye shadow.

"That's where I met my second husband. Jack Sullivan. He worked in the glass factory and bowled on the men's league on the same night we did. After our three games, we'd return our shoes and meet the guys in the bowling alley bar every Wednesday night. Jack was funny. He told the best dirty jokes."

"Really." Hootie sipped his beer. It tasted flat.

"One night, I had a little too much to drink. A month later, I'm puking my guts out at work thinking, 'Oh shit, I got the flu.' I didn't have the flu."

Hootie turned the page. Brenda and Jack's wedding day. Brenda wore a mint-green dress with matching eye shadow. Jack had on a wrinkled brown suit which hung on his skinny frame. On the front of his belt, he sported a pewter buckle plate the size of his fist. It displayed the profile of a deer head with majestic antlers. Something to the right of the camera had caught Jack's attention just as the shutter opened. Both the deer and Jack appeared to look in the same direction. Brenda faced the camera with a polite smile.

"My sisters threw me a baby shower." She pointed to the party snapshot. "And here is my pride and joy." Brenda lay her head on Hootie's shoulder.

Hootie looked at the tiny pink child. Jolene, four-days-old.

"She's beautiful," he said. "Is she supposed to be that red?"

"Maybe she was filling her diaper. Let me go check on dinner." Brenda rushed birdlike toward the kitchen, elbows at her side and hands flapping outward.

Hootie turned the page. A snapshot showed Brenda's hair cut short and dyed dark brown, her plucked eyebrows two tense lines. She was pregnant again. She stood in front of a rusty maroon Monte Carlo. Jolene, with matted hair, stood at Brenda's side. Then the next snapshot: Betsy, three-days-old. Two beautiful girls. Hootie traced the snapshot of the newborn baby's face with his finger. He and his ex-wife never had children.

Hootie turned the page. Summer day at the lake. Brenda's girls played with a beach ball in the foreground. They wore pink and yellow ruffled bathing suits. They both had their mother's golden hair. Unfortunately, their father's big ears protruded from their small heads like sails. In the background, Brenda sat alone in an Adirondack chair wearing sunglasses and a long-sleeve shirt.

Easter Sunday. Brenda and the girls bedecked in identical dresses and gloves. The girls wore white brimmed bonnets with elastic bands under their chins. The three of them posed politely for the camera. The next was an action shot. Devilish Betsy had pulled Jolene's bonnet elastic and was ready to snap. Jolene had the look of terror in her eyes. Brenda shouted at the girls.

Hootie looked at the snapshot again. Brenda looked tired. Dark circles under her eyes gave her a haunted appearance. Who took these pictures? Did Jack go to church with them? Did she raise the girls on her own?

Hootie turned the page. Betsy's seventh birthday. Brenda's parents' kitchen. Betsy smiled behind a flaming birthday cake, Brenda leaning against the countertop. Her hair was cropped short again, bleach-blonde. She looked to have lost even more weight. She did not wear a wedding ring.

Hootie turned the page. Brenda and Big John's wedding day.

"Big John? Who the hell is Big John?" He sipped the warm beer. Another Justice of the Peace wedding. Deep creases carved the sides of Brenda's mouth. She stood smiling next to the tall cowboy named John.

"She doesn't give up. I'll give her that."

Christmas 1976. The girls threw tinsel on the tree and waved at the camera. Big John sat on the couch, still wearing his cowboy boots, his feet propped on the coffee table. He stared at the TV.

Hootie scanned the holiday pictures, birthday pictures, graduation pictures. Brenda wore a wedding ring, but Big John was nowhere to be found.

Betsy's graduation party. Betsy looked much older than she was in her black miniskirt, big hoop earrings, and heavy eye makeup. Her hair was dark brown. Betsy lifted a bottle of beer towards the camera and smiled dazedly. She looked drunk.

Mom and Dad's in their new Florida house. A kind elderly couple stood in front of an orange tree in the front yard of a double-wide. *They look so sweet,* Hootie thought. Could these people actually be related?

The next snapshot: My new home! Brenda posed in front of her current trailer. The Disney Christmas tree stood in the corner of the patio.

Hootie turned he page. Brenda and George's wedding.

"Jesus Christ." Hootie massaged his temples. "How many does that make? Four?" He looked at the picture again. Skinny Brenda in a lavender dress dwarfed by fat George in his rust-colored corduroy suit and wide white tie. Brenda in the next snapshot opened presents from her friends. Someone gave her a towel set which read: *Hers and Theirs.* The caption on the bottom of the picture read: *Ha-Ha. Very funny!*

Hootie jumped up and sat on the arm of the sofa. How could that carefree little eight-year-old farm girl turn into Brenda? How could she make so many wrong choices? He felt sorry for her. He wanted to help her. He wanted to run screaming and never look back. He closed the photo album.

Hootie turned and looked at the front door. He heard the buzz of the oven alarm.

"Dinner's ready." Brenda appeared in the living room doorway, wiping her hands on her apron, bracelets rattling. "I hope you like meatloaf." She disappeared back into the kitchen.

"Yeah."

THE GIFT OF WHAT FOR

DANIEL DAMIANO

It was only a matter of time. Eventually, I knew what a certain ring on my phone would symbolize. "He can go any day, so you might want to…," my stepmother trailed off.

We didn't know each other well. They were married shortly before things permanently soured with my father and me. She always seemed nice enough. Teri had been married before. Her previous husband had died a few years prior. She met my father at the grocery store, when he was complaining aloud in the frozen foods section that he couldn't cook. Teri, in her adjacent kindness, offered some handy, simple recipes that would fit a disheveled widower like a glove, which was probably little more than mixing a type of meat with a type of pasta or cheese sauce.

To hear her tell it at their wedding, such culinary Samaritanism would lead to a date and, within months, a proposal. They were now married for about three years. I imagined that, if nothing else, they would keep each other from the loneliness that came with the deaths of their spouses. Most of their marriage I had been removed from their lives. It certainly wasn't Teri's fault. My father was my father, and that was always why. He was my father when my mother was alive and, when she was, his head smacks and verbal swipes were somewhat diverted from causing blunt force trauma, even if they still stung. When mom died, even though I was thirty-seven, his insults felt all the more potent without her attempted assurances that my father didn't mean the things he said.

After my mother passed, I still lived nearby and would feel obligated to have contact with my father, based purely on the fact that I was the sole offspring. I was saddled with the inevitable *how could I abandon lonely dad*, even if my visits continually reduced what little self-esteem I was clinging to.

"The world eats up people like you," he'd say. "Failure dies alone, and you're headin' there," was another one. I could only be thankful he never wrote for fortune cookies. My father didn't take kind to aspiring artists, as I was. If you weren't a manager of something by thirty-five, you were a loser. If you weren't married with kids—gay. And if you were a manager of something, married, a father...and *actually* gay, well, you'd still be gay but also ostracized.

I could be little else but him.

Still with the phone in my hand, as Teri gave details of my father's current state, I was transported back to the lacerating barbs that always led to my depression, especially as a teenager. He could do it in a breakfast, like an emotionally-draining magician—in less than a half-hour, between the first coffee sip and the last forkful of scrambled eggs, I was reduced to a mass of quivering uncertainty. After many such character eviscerations, I was often fraught with: "What if he's right?"

Growing up, I remembered my mother's consolations, which were always out of his earshot: "He loves you. He just doesn't understand you." And always in hushed tones, as if we were in church. Yes, she was a little scared of him. It made me wonder just how I managed to be conceived by my parents, since I never saw them even touch. It made more sense that I was simply handed to them by a trench-coated stranger as a sort of runner-up black market baby.

He was a lion of a man, with a receding mane, whom one didn't argue with. Over the years, I watched his only brother, my Uncle Ken, get devoured at holiday dinners if he, in any way, brought forth a counter argument to my father's complaints at society's failings, usually blaming some covert liberal faction. My father would metaphorically bring out the snow shovel and bury Uncle Ken in a mass of accrued pseudo-knowledge that reduced a smart man, as my Uncle Ken was, to some boob who obtained information solely by eavesdropping on subway conversations.

So many Thanksgivings and Christmases I watched Uncle Ken, a Philosophy major no less, leave a little shorter and more hunched than when he arrived, as my father stewed in his living room chair watching football, oblivious of the toxins he'd managed to fertilize the festivities with. I increasingly pitied Uncle Ken as I got older before eventually realizing, especially after he died of a massive heart attack at fifty-eight on a subway platform, that I was becoming him. I too felt weakened and hunched by my father's sheer presence and was sure to become more debilitated with time if something didn't change.

Teri was still speaking into my one ear, as the past whispered in my other. From my father, I heard "loser," "idiot," "nobody," "nobody," "nobody." From Teri, I could only hear "malignant," "breathing labored," "any day," "any day," "any day…"

She gave a room number and the hospital where my dad was at, and I thanked her. I didn't tell her when I would be going, only that I would. I would need to ponder when, but obviously didn't have all the time in the world. I would've been fine with arriving when it was too late; at least I could say I'd made the effort. But knowing this man as I did, I knew he'd linger like a fart under a bedsheet. I could see it all: the doctor's perplexity at how he still hung on, the staff inquiring with Teri if he had any unresolved issues with family, her pleading messages on my answering machine underscored with his labored breathing in the background. Dear God…

Wanting to rip off the band-aid of awkwardness sooner than later, I took the train from my Astoria, Queens apartment to Bay Ridge the next morning. I couldn't eat. Even oxygen seemed gluttonous. My stomach was filled with nerves bubbling like shaken seltzer, a feeling transcending the most nervous I had ever been in my life—when I performed open mics at comedy clubs, which never got easier, even after doing over thirty of them. Now all those times I waited offstage, petrified yet envious of the snickers barely earned by the previous acts, running my material in my head *ad nauseum*, paled by comparison to this train ride to Brooklyn. And yet it was fitting that I drew the comparison, since my stand-up act would prove to be the reason for the permanent severing of our relationship.

The worst it could get for a struggling stand-up comedian was when you spotted a parent in the audience whom you already had strained relations with. This could only be topped, of course, by that parent's departure just thirty seconds into your ten-minute set.

"Anyone here have a parent that sucks the frigging life out of you? Show of hands?" This began my routine on that fateful night at the aptly named "Grungy's Comedy Dungeon." I caught his eyes. *Why is he here?* I thought, while stammering through the next few lines of my routine. *Why the hell are you here?* I asked, internally, the spotlight now seeming to weigh on my face like a falling comet, as the beads of sweat cascaded down my cheeks and over my lips. I was all but a waterfall attempting to tell jokes about my boorish father. The silence that followed was filled only by his footsteps leaving the club.

I bombed that night, which was the understatement of the year. I melted. I all but disintegrated on stage before a packed club. I fumbled and flop-sweated my way to a merciful black-out and swift exit offstage, greeted by the *sucks-to-be-you* looks from my fellow comedians. It would be my last time performing stand-up, which wasn't the worst thing. At the time, I thought if I had to quit, better the incentive be a catastrophic performance of unparalleled proportions. I didn't even particularly care if my father was insulted and if he never spoke to me again. As it turned out, this was the best way to sever ties. In the half-minute of my routine that he witnessed, I managed to convey my honest feelings about him better than I ever could in life. I needed a microphone to give me the courage to verbalize his stifling impact.

It did dawn on me that if he wasn't there, and I was able to go through my routine as planned, I may have "killed," as they say. Hell, there were talent agents in the audience, I was told. It may have been what cracked the glass for me as a stand-up performer. Or not. In any case, it didn't seem meant to be.

And yet what exactly *was* to be?

Perhaps my finally being free of him. Maybe to have this moment for me to see him dying, and for his eyes to just squint enough to see my face as he left the Earth on the wings of guilt for his treatment of me, of my mother, of Uncle Ken, of so many. He did it all wrong. He paid the mortgage and thought that warranted his tyranny. He was lucky he had a second wife who gave a shit. Three years without me as his punching bag, and now he had one thing coming: my...*vindication?* And what kind, exactly? I was still single, living with a pain-in-the-ass roommate, struggling to pay bills,...but I did leave the borough. I was out of his eyeshot, and still kept writing stories and poems, with occasional nibbles but, granted, few bites. I guess I would still be considered a failure in his eyes, but what'd he know of my life? For three years, not a call, an e-mail. No other family to inform him of what I was up to. He had no way of knowing that...I hadn't accomplished much more than he'd said I would.

But I was alive,...and he was dying. I had the edge.

Suddenly, this arduous train ride was becoming more pleasurable as I took in the East River from the Brooklyn Bridge. I wasn't afraid. I was only anxious. Anxious to give him what for—a term often used by my father, passed down from his father. Whenever he bragged about telling off the subordinates at his job or bureaucrats or...even harmless cashiers or telemarketers, he'd say, "I sure gave him what for, I'll tell ya'."

"What for" was somewhat of an old school term for a verbal whipping. *It'd be nice to be on the other side of it, for a change,* I thought. And I wouldn't care who heard me. Yes, I was going to gleefully stand over his deathbed and give my old man what for because the asshole deserved it.

I entered the cold, sterile hallways of St. Vic's Hospital, assured that I would not allow my father's feeble health to dilute my adrenaline. I knew exactly what I wanted to say. I entered the room in the ICU on the fourth floor, Room 405D, and there he was, alone with the curtain pulled to mask his upper body, revealing only his hand and covered lower extremities. But that hand was enough. I remembered the things that right hand did, and it wasn't shaking mine. The whacks across the back of my head, the grabbing of my mother, the punches in walls, the swigs of too many beers after a distressing workday.

Yes, I could tell that hand anywhere. It hadn't changed a day.

No one was around as I sat beside his bed. Only the occasional beeps from the machinery attached to him, but otherwise, a respectful audience. And so I began the routine I never got to finish on that fateful night, three years ago:

"Hey, anyone here have a parent that sucks the frigging life out of you? Show of hands?" I said in a nearly guttural rasp. Of course the one hand present in the room, other than my own, could not be raised, as I looked down at his worn knuckles. "No? Well, allow me to break the ice. I have one. My father. My father is the Hoover Vacuum of parents. You got a few crumbs of optimism inside you, he'll find 'em and suck 'em right out. Oh, yes. If you ever had any sense of self-worth around my father, within minutes, you'd find yourself with the morale of a sixteen-year-old nerd with a locker room wedgie. My father basically thinks that if you can live a few moments of a day void of utter misery, you need to be committed. This from a man who up until I was about ten could not use a fork with one hand without slapping me with the other. As a kid, breakfast with my father was always like dining with a grizzly bear. He would just randomly eat, grunt, and swipe at my head. I musta' been the only kid in my neighborhood who ate Cheerios with a helmet and mace. For years, I found I couldn't eat anything without flinching. My life was like a strange sense-memory experiment. If I was eating soup, I ducked. And this is when I ate alone. In restaurants, these out of context spasms must've generated sympathy! Probably why I always got free dessert!"

At this point, my volume had risen to the operatic, undaunted by the gathering taps of nurses' sneakers at the doorway, until I got to the end:

"You…you son of a – " I swiped the curtain open, my impatience finally summoning the strength to venture off-script and curse him out to his face, only to find that the face I was looking at…was a woman's. And not just a woman, and one I obviously didn't know in the slightest, but one who actually was…laughing. I wasn't even delivering it well. I was so angry. I didn't have any of the honed comedic style I'd developed over thirty pathetic open mics. But, my God, this was the best reaction I'd ever had. I was killing! Almost literally.

The nurses came running in and tended to her, as if I were invisible, as the woman continued to laugh uproariously, which sounded like the first conscious breaths she had uttered in days. I didn't know whether to apologize or continue to bathe in the adulation. It was so strange to be torn in such a way, pulled by guilt of this patient's possible death and a performer's need for acceptance.

"HAH! HAH! HAH! HAH!" she continued, stripping her worn sixty-some-year-old vocal chords, as the nurses furiously tried to sit her up so she wouldn't choke. "HAH! HAH! HAH! HAH!" She started to cough, "CUH! CUH! CUUUUUUUUUUH," which grew to a disturbing caterwaul followed by asthmatic wheezing. She looked at me with bulged eyes, now clearly in despair as the nurses looked at me with contempt for thrusting them into a near code blue.

"I'm...I'm so... I didn't mean...," I stammered as I discreetly back-pedaled. By the time I got to the doorway, it thankfully appeared the poor woman had come out of her coughing and wheezing spell and had now gone back to laughing. But, at this point, it was neither a good nor a bad thing.

I just needed to leave.

I stepped out into the hall, a few feet from the nurses' station, now feeling like I was lost in a sterile town. I had the room number etched into my brain from when Teri had given it to me over the phone. *Did they move him? Did he already pass?*

As I approached the nurses' desk, "Excuse me. I'm here to see —"

"Chris?" Teri appeared at the end of the counter, with a weakened smile.

"Teri?"

"It's good to see you, Chris," she said, sincerely.

"You too." We awkwardly hugged. "How are you, considering...?"

"I'm okay. You know, it's not easy. He doesn't have long. It's good you're here."

We looked at each other, not knowing each other well enough to go beyond this, until it dawned on me that I still didn't know where he was.

"Um, where is he? I went to 405D and —"

"D? Oh, no. It's B. I thought I said, 'B-as-in-Boy' on the phone, but maybe I..."

"No, that's fine, Teri. You probably did and I just misheard you."

"So you went to 405D?" she said, with severity.

"Uh, yeah, but it's...It's fine."

"I'm sorry."

"Teri, there's nothing to be sorry about. B and D, hey, it happens, right?" I grinned, attempting to incur one from Teri, but this amusing error, given the circumstances, appeared far too serious for her to find humor. In truth, I'm sure Teri did make it very clear, and I was simply distracted by my father's voice in my other ear. It was a wonder I'd made it to the right hospital, considering all that was running through my mind during that call, the famed chorus: "loser," "idiot," "nobody," "nobody," "nobody…"

"Why don't you go in?" Teri brought me back to Earth. "He's not speaking anymore, and he's in and out of consciousness, but I'm sure he'll sense you."

"Do you want to be with him a little more by yourself? I can wait out here."

"No, you go. I've been here since last night, and I have to stop by my apartment to feed Ringo."

"Ringo?"

"Oh, that's my dog. I got him a few months ago."

"Oh. Cool."

She smiled at this, then it registered with me, "Um, your apartment? Did Dad sell the house?"

"Oh. No, he…he still has it, Chris. We…Well, I may as well tell you, your father and I split up about six months ago."

"Really? Wha…Divorced?"

"Mm-hm." She reluctantly nodded.

"I'm…I had…Wow, I…"

"It's okay. But, yeah."

I knew it was okay, of course. The question was why, but I knew that answer as well. It was pointless to ask. Teri was a nice person, as my mother was. My father wasn't. And apparently a newly married life at a late age wasn't softening him.

He was still…him.

"Does he know I'm coming?" I weakly asked.

"No. I don't think he even knows he's in a hospital at this point, Chris."

I sat with this, before Teri assured, "I'll be back in a couple of hours. If you're not here, I'll keep you informed of things."

She walked off, as I remained. *This doesn't feel right,* I thought.

I instinctively ran toward Teri, who now stood in front of a closed elevator door.

"Teri?"

She looked at me, clearly not knowing what I would suggest.

"Look, take your time. I'm...I'll put myself as the point of contact, if you'd like. You shouldn't have to deal with all this now."

"No, Chris. That's...I can..."

I could tell in her tone that she would concede but felt it would be less painful for her as an ex-wife than for me as the estranged son to deal with the handling of my father's last days. *What a position he put us in,* I thought. He drove away a lovely woman, who now felt obligated to him because he drove away his only son. It still didn't seem right.

"Teri, please, I'll handle it. I'll have them contact me and I'll keep you in the loop with everything, okay?"

"You sure?" she asked, knowing this wasn't easy.

"Yeah, please. I appreciate what you've done."

"Chris, I didn't do anything."

"You married him. That was more than he deserved."

"Chris, don't say that."

"It's true, Teri. I know that sonofabitch."

"Chris..."

"Teri, I *know* him. I've known him my whole life. I'm sorry, but you don't need to defend him to me. Okay?"

I was more assertive with Teri than I had anticipated, but at a certain point I just knew it could only be me and him. He was part of what had brought me into the world, so it seemed only fair I see him out of it.

"Chris, I don't know if you ever knew, but I told him to go see you perform that night. I thought it'd be good for him to see you in your...creative element, but...I guess it wasn't."

"That's okay," as I took this in.

"I told him to call you afterwards, but he just...He was...upset."

"Did he ever say anything about it?"

"I asked. He just...put up his hand. I think it was the only time he didn't have something to say." She couldn't help but grin, if painfully, at this.

"Huh." I returned a weak smile.

"I've always felt bad, Chris."

"Why?"

"I know he was hard on you…I just thought…it'd do something for him to see you doing what you loved, especially since he never saw you do it. But…it wasn't my place."

"Teri, you have nothing to apologize for."

She smiled at this, but it wasn't one of confidence. More one of regret and sadness, as if for a reason beyond this.

She continued, "We made mistakes with my son, my first husband and I. And I thought…Well, sometimes you learn late, as a parent,…and then it's too late. It was for him." She sat with this. It dawned on me that her son must've killed himself. I had no idea. *What was his father like?* I thought. Or maybe it wasn't like that.

She then smiled as she looked off, regretfully. "Your father and I weren't a very good married couple. But I wouldn't just blame your father. I said yes. I should've known."

"That he was an asshole?" I only half-joked.

She looked at me, almost willing to agree, then followed, "We were both lonely people in the end, Chris. But that's not enough. Even when you're older."

I gave Teri credit for not cashing in her remaining years with such a man as my father. If she was unhappy, she should've left him, as she did. And yet she was still here, willing to handle all of this crap, because there was no one else. I then started to wonder if their marriage would have lasted if I were around. Or would it have ended even sooner? Was I the only reason my mother stuck around?

I guess it didn't matter.

In the end, I could only be thankful to Teri. If it wasn't for her, he would've never ventured to Grungy's Comedy Dungeon and heard how I really felt about him. It was a stupid stand-up routine, but what little he heard, he must've known stemmed from truth. He probably went with the intent of affirming I was on a useless path, and instead came away ashamed, which he could only reveal by resentful silence. And I wasn't going to extend myself or apologize because, in truth, I didn't want to. I didn't want anything to do with the man anymore. I was happy to not see him even for obligatory holidays. I was happy to just not see him. Now his dying was the lame excuse for our reunion. And he was alone, to boot. Fortunate to have the presence of his ex-wife, who no doubt pitied him just as she did when they met in the frozen foods section, when he complained aloud about his culinary deficiencies.

As Teri took the elevator down, my anger at my father had resurfaced. But now it didn't seem right to repeat my embittered three-year-old stand-up bit, especially after it had done so well in room 405D. Now it just seemed anti-climactic.

But I could still give him what for. *Oh, yes.*

I would just go into the room, see him lying there, and unleash my parting gift to him. It may not have the polish of a routine, but it would suffice.

I walked into 405B, and there he was, eyes closed, thin, ashen, head tilted towards the window which viewed St. Anthony's Church across the street. The eyes of Jesus on the façade looked inside at me, as if eagerly awaiting my histrionic display. I peered over at my father, as I had envisioned myself doing on the train ride in, looked down at his right hand, which had the emaciated scaliness of an old sturgeon. Weak and harmless. The woman in 405D actually looked more like my father as I remembered him than my father did now. But I knew this was the man I had grown to hate, resent, was tormented and reduced by.

This was him, the prick.

I continued my gaze at his tired face and closed eyes. "Dad?" I asked. He didn't so much as flinch. "I know you can hear me, okay? It's Chris."

Again, not a flinch, only his labored exhales which sounded like distant waves.

I looked out again at the inquisitive Jesus, then off through the door at the passing nurses and the squeaks of gurney wheels, then back at my father.

I was reminded of the edge I had. The one thing I had over him now — I was living. But then I realized it was less an edge I had over him than something I simply needed to be aware of. Yes, I was living. *So what do I do with this?*

Does my life peak at telling off my father on his deathbed?

I looked down at the infamous right hand, the bear claw that knew the back of my head more than the hair that grew out of it. I touched it, as I looked at him, realizing its harsh capabilities were a thing of the past. I then squeezed it, gently.

And in his semi-conscious state, I felt just the slightest squeeze in return.

SDS, INC.

JIM MOSS

From: The Office of Mr. Sloth
Re: Retirement Party, Friday, May 30th, 9:00 PM, The
Roasted Bull, 114 Wall Street.

Mr. Sloth would like to thank all of you for your hard work
this past year, and also apologize for being unable attend his
upcoming early retirement party due to commitments in
Tahiti. You'll be happy to know that Ms. Gluttony, the new
Director of Operations, has decided not to cancel the party
and graciously ordered additional food and refreshments
for everyone's enjoyment. So please remember to attend. I'm
sure we will all miss Mr. Sloth's carefree demeanor and
skillful delegation of projects, and fondly recall the many
exhilarating evenings our team worked overtime to meet
deadlines while Mr. Sloth directed, via conference call, from
the company sauna.

It has been a challenging year for SDS, Inc. since our
founder, Godrick Pride, left to pursue bigger opportunities.
We have managed to weather the public scandals
concerning Chairman Wrath's assault conviction, and the
numerous sexual harassment allegations filed against Vice
President Lust. Fortunately, under the leadership of our
new CEO, Mr. Avarice, profits continue to rise, and the year
ahead promises to be a banner one.

Sadly, due to Mr. Sloth's departure, my position here will be
discontinued. No additional job terminations are planned,
so you can all continue to enjoy your opulent lifestyles
without having to worry about looking for employment or
selling your vacation homes. Yes, please, savor your high-
rise luxury apartments, your overly generous stock options
and those personal loans the company so readily makes

available to its top executives. After all, you deserve your success, due to the merit of being raised in an upscale suburb with quality schools and well-to-do parents who can afford to send you to prestigious universities where you can earn those respected degrees to acquire high-paying jobs. Don't concern yourself with us underlings. We'll scrape out a living with the puny severance packages and paltry 401-K's this Fortune 500 Cor-poor-ration has so generously provided us.

Bitter Regards,

Constance Envy
Former Administrative Assistant

LISA'S GONE

RORY PENLAND

Robert walked onto the back porch, overlooking the open field behind his modest farmhouse. He had just finished washing the dishes. He dried his hands with a dishtowel, but the evening breeze told him they were still moist. It was dark-early because of daylights savings time. He hated how it got dark at six now.

He heard the familiar hoot owl which had made a home for itself in his leaning red barn. He'd braced it, but it was still a tad lopsided. The red paint had faded but wasn't exactly pink. Robert was winsome since losing his wife. It wasn't fair that he'd lost his beloved at so young an age in their relationship. They hadn't even spent twenty years together before she had been taken from him.

They had known each other since they were toddlers. Such was the way in small places in the country. Everybody knew everybody and they all knew each other's business. They played together as kids, went to high school prom with each other, and kissed behind her Daddy's barn. It wasn't long before they got married. They never had children—Lisa was "barren" (as she used to always say, and he hated that term). Robert (who never liked to be called "Bob") loved her so very much and he was happy just to be with her.

Dogs and other animals came and went in their lives. The owl in the barn had arrived just a few years before Lisa had gone to that great place in the sky. Lisa had loved that owl, not just because it killed the rats in that dusty old barn, but because she thought the way it sounded was magical. She always perked up when she heard it. And so Robert always nodded when it hooted loud, letting him know he was never totally alone.

Before Lisa's journey to the heavens, they did have their fair share of ups and downs. He farmed for a while but found he wasn't very good at it. He rotated his crops, turned the soil, and fertilized it as was the mandate of the *Farmers' Almanacs*. There were just too many variables he hadn't counted on, especially the unpredictable weather of southernmost Georgia.

He managed to get a job selling tractors and seemed to have "found his calling," as Lisa put it. "He can sell sand to an Arab and ice to an Eskimo," she would often say. This success helped them buy their first pick-up truck which was unfortunately a lemon. A gasket blown here, a burnt taillight there.

Then came the doctor visit where Lisa was told she could never bear a child. The months after were emotionally fraught. So much crying! Robert gave many needed hugs of reassurance and, though their love for each other was tested to the limit, they eventually made it through the ordeal together.

Their favorite past time on the weekends was going to the six-plex movie theater in town. They would buy a big bucket of popcorn and Robert would eat most of it before the picture even started. She liked dramas and romance while he preferred action and science fiction movies. Those were always good times for them. They could cuddle and escape to somewhere else. Some other place far away from their mundane ordinary stale country life. But those times together were long gone now, replaced by a vast dark empty void.

This was his time to gaze up at the open sky, to listen to the wind as it rustled the trees and tall grass of the field. More importantly — it was his time for talking with Lisa. He looked upwards and spoke: "I hope wherever you are up there…you are at peace, sweetheart. I miss you something fierce." He was surprised at how old his own voice sounded. He swallowed hard and walked out towards the field. A few minutes into the tall grass, he looked up again. "I wish there was some way I could join you right now." He paused, tears streaming his cheeks. "I know I say that every time I come out here. Almost every day since…"

A bright light shone down on him from the once dark sky. He felt the warmth of the light and his skin tingled. At long last they had returned. His prayer to the sky had finally been answered. Robert disappeared as if he had never been there, and the sky went dark again. In the barn, the old owl hooted calmly.

What happened next was a kaleidoscope of weirdness: Robert found himself on a long table looking upwards at strange, unearthly lights. He was completely paralyzed. The fringes of his vision were fuzzy. A pair of aliens looked over him. He's always imagined they

78

would be green, but they were more of a yellow-brownish color. Their heads were smooth and bulbous, containing large dark eyes. Their mouths and noses were very small in contrast to their heads.

One alien moved Robert's head from side to side, giving him a quick view of another two tables. One table held a large goat while the other contained a small girl, also lying with her eyes open, looking straight up. She seemed frozen as Robert was. He looked at his captors again. They were concentrating on him now. In his mind there was something strange about the girl he had just seen, but the view had been so fast, literally a split second.

Robert knew a lot about alien abduction. He had read up a lot on the subject after Lisa got taken. Many claimed they had been experimented on, but they had all been brought back. Why had they not brought Lisa back? Did they take her to another planet for further study? Was she in some sort of intergalactic zoo somewhere? Did she die?

The aliens hovered over him. One examiner brought an instrument to Robert's forehead and he felt a sharp pain between his eyes. Things happened to his vision. Everything looked greenish, then everything looked red. Sound became muffled, though he could not feel anything in or around his ears.

The alien retracted with the sinister needle-tipped instrument. The other held up a large, ominous, gun-like apparatus. It became leveled at Robert's left side. A severe pain shot up Robert's shoulder to the center of his brain. These scientists from another world had worked out how to immobilize creatures for study but had little concern for how to anesthetize them! Robert looked again and saw what was wrong with the little girl next to him—her legs had been carefully dissected and separated just above her kneecaps. His pain became so unbearable, blackness knocked Robert out quickly. During the whole process, he could feel every moment of his left arm being surgically lasered and pulled apart just above his elbow.

He awoke with a start. He was out in the field, lying on smooshed grass. He could smell the grass his body had pushed over. He looked around, dazed. Had he fallen in the field? He slowly rose to his feet. What time was it? He gingerly walked his way back to the farmhouse. He stepped onto the back porch and looked back at the field again. Why was he out there? He hadn't been drinking. A light went on upstairs, casting a dim glow over the ground behind the house. He heard someone bounding down the stairs. Lisa came out the back door from the kitchen and hugged him.

"I was so worried," she said lovingly.

Robert hugged her back. "Why?" he asked.

She gave him a serious look. "I woke up out in the field. I didn't know how I got out there. I came in and you were nowhere to be found. That was hours ago." The two walked back into the house together. The clock on the kitchen wall said 5:20.

"I just woke up out there, too," he said, confused. "I can't figure it out. I know you're here and I'm here, but I have this strange feeling, like I've been missing you for a long time."

Lisa gave her man a tender smile, making his eyebrows raise. "I can't explain any of it. It's weird." She kissed his cheek. "We're not old enough to be getting senile yet."

The loving couple went upstairs, and Robert made love to his better half like he had never made love to her before. They listened to the barn owl as they watched the sun come up in each other's arms, then made love again.

In the following weeks, the two were further confounded by some of the locals insisting Lisa had been missing for months. Stranger yet, her doctor told them it was a miracle but she, aged forty, was pregnant—with twins! Robert and Lisa couldn't figure any of it out. They decided to just thank the powers that be from above for their blessings.

FUDGE

JIM MOSS

My Daddy didn't want to live that way and wasn't going to live that way. That was his wish. That's why I got to get custody. Billy Ray will kill 'em. He's made that clear. He's lyin' about Daddy's last words. Lyin.' He hates Fudge. Always called him "that shit brown mutt." And Fudge is a purebred lab. No! He's lyin,' I was there! Look, two weeks before it all happened, Daddy said he wanted to die. Right after the doctor told him he'd likely be paralyzed from the neck down for the rest of his life. They'd do all they could. Therapy and so such. But three specialists told him the same thing. Then last week Doctor Cabbers told Daddy they expected to get him off the breathin' machine in a week. Daddy told the doctor, "Don't bother waitin' a week. Just pull the plug right now."

Doctor laughed 'cause he thought Daddy was kiddin,' but Daddy wasn't kiddin.' Doctors said Daddy was depressed. They wanted him to want to live. That's why they allowed Fudge to visit, animals being able to lift people's spirits and such. I'd have to lift Daddy's arm and work his hand so's he could pet Fudge. Weird pettin' a dog with someone else's hand. Got real tiring...

It was Fudge's third visit. Daddy spent two hours just talkin' to Fudge. Not to us...just the dog. Then Daddy calls us over and says to us humans, me and Billy Ray, he says, "You make sure to take good care of Fudge. You. Take. Good care. Of him." That was his last words to us. Then he said he wanted time alone to talk to Fudge.

I hooked the leash to the bed and Bobby an' I went out in the hall, keepin' the door cracked open, mind ya, to keep an eye on them. And Daddy's talkin' to Fudge, then Daddy says, "Git me stick, boy. Git me stick." And Fudge starts lookin' around and whinin' 'cause there ain't no sticks in the room. But Daddy keeps insistin,' "Git me stick." And son-of-a-gun if that dog don't pick up and start yankin' on the cable handlin' Daddy's life support.

Before we could do anything, he'd yanked it right out of the wall. All these alarms and buzzers start going off. We yell for the nurse. And Daddy! Daddy, with his last breath says, "Kill, Fudge." Yes, I know! But he said that to Fudge! Not to us. Because as soon as he said it, these hackles appear on Fudge's back and he starts growlin' at us. And this, mind ya, this is a dog that loves strangers, that wags his tail and slobbers kisses on everyone he meets. Fudge wouldn't let anyone near Daddy. Neither me nor Billy Ray, and he 'bout near tore Billy's hand off...He was snarlin' and a lungin' at anyone who got close.

Finally, this male nurse comes in with a blanket to throw on him and this doctor's got a syringe ready, but by that time, Daddy was dead. Fudge just laid down at the foot of the bed, whimpering. Well, now you got him. The state's got him. Call him what you want. A dog that killed one man and bit another man's finger off. But that ain't the way most people see it. You need to grant me custody. Read the papers. Read the editorials. You can't euthanize Fudge!

THE GOOD CAT

VICKI HENDRICKS

I had no name till Dad took me home. Now I answer to "Lickrish," "Buddy," and "Son"—when I feel like it. I gave up chasing lizards, squirrels, and birds, and climbing trees, for Dad. None of it was as good as his fingers behind my ears, his soft belly-lap, and the tang of his silky armpit slung across our bedsheets where I curl. I am a good boy till I start trouble.

Dad is on the couch and I am in his lap, as we are supposed to be at night. He turns my head toward his snout. "Son," he says, his fingers massaging the tingly spot above my tail, "you're the only one Dad needs." I stretch forward, head down, butt up. I hunker into a cuddly lump and purr, keeping my eyes cracked on a swaying palm frond outside the window. I'm lulled by the movement—*happy*—as Dad calls it. He rests his hand on my back and watches the picture-screen.

After a while he says, "Buddy, let's take a drive to my Ami. Wanna?" It is a place with windows in the sky, a world of sand, and salty waves that try to drown you if you stop to dig a hole. I leap to his shoulder and tuck my forepaws into the dark stubble on his neck, scouring the side of his face with my tongue till he pulls me off. He does not understand what I am telling him, that we are happy on the couch. I do not want to go to his Ami, or anywhere, but I do not want to stay home all by myself.

He brings my hard cave from the closet, and I dart inside, bracing, so not to be flung against the metal bars as he carries me to the engine-car. When I am beside him on the seat, he pokes a finger through the bars. "Son, we got us a sweet one tonight. I been watching her and waiting a long time. Hell, . . . they're all sweet."

I was small, weak, and hungry when I found Dad. I had a sore haunch, bit by a nasty raccoon that wanted to fight over a greasy Mac wrapper. I fed on dry lizards and rancid Mac scraps—a juicy mouse, almost never. I got drenched in storms and would have been flattened by engine-cars if I were not so smart.

I did not know any other place, just the building with metal tables outside, grass, concrete, and hot salty wind. Mamma hid me under bushes till she went away. I kept my distance from people, but Dad lured me with crumbles of fresh Mac. I rubbed my bony raised-back against his lower hind leg to ask for more, and he scooped me up. Now I sleep safe on the couch during daylight. When my stomach starts to grind, Dad comes home for feeding-time. I get *pâté* or morsels in rich gravy.

One night when I was new, Dad loaded his backpack and went off without me. I hiked a pee on the door. I am a silent kitty, except for a tiny squeak, so it was my only way to show hurt feelings. The next time he left at night, he locked me in my cave. I made sick all over and licked it off my fur and brought it up again. When Dad got home, I was foul.

"You're breaking my heart, Son." He put me into the sink with soap like I was a dirty pan, but the water was warm, and afterwards he rubbed me dry. I looked into his eyes and squeaked. He knew I wanted to go with him, and I would be his good boy.

The engine-car stops, and my cave is lifted out under a low tree. I am bumped side to side through darkness, following a light dot with Dad. My cave is set solid while Dad digs into his pack and clanks tools above me. I hear snapping and smell rubber hand covers that I have seen Dad bring home. Powder drifts into my cage and I sneeze.

I sniff sand and grass, and close by . . . pee. This pee is ripe with female. It tugs at my belly, a feeling of want. The sweet one? Is she for me?

I tunnel at the corner of my cave, but my claws click without traction. I am tilted upward near the face of Dad and slide back, hitting the wall. He has a white cover over his snout and colorful cloth down to his brows. I would not know him except for his scent. He looks into my eyes and shushes me. I fly against the grate as he dips me down again near the pee perfume. I tunnel wildly with no progress.

Something clicks and slides above me. Cool, dry air drops human female scent inside my cave. I am lifted indoors. My eyes can see everything, but Dad follows the light dot into a room with a couch and sets my cave on the floor. He has brought my favorite, rabbit *pâté*, and lets me out to feed. I lick it to be nice until he moves away. This is all new territory that I need to explore. My nose untangles waves of human and sharp soap scent, like the smell of Dad when he comes home at feeding-time. It fades. Dad has closed off the smell without making a sound.

Under the table, I nose a few hard crumbs and a fragment of cheese. I lick it up. I circle the room and sniff all the corners and under the couch. Just dust, no threats. Pee scent creeps out from under the shut door where Dad has gone. It is human female pee. Dad must have that feeling of want.

I follow a scent of grease to the kitchen, but there is no food I can find. I go to my rabbit *pâté*, finish, and take a quick bath. Time for a nap. I leap to a chair with a soft pillow and knead it into shape. Not cuddly like the lap of Dad.

Whining comes from the other room. I slink close. I listen. It is human noise. I sniff fear. Dad opens up. There is a face in the dark, white stuffing sticking from her mouth. Dad rolls out a chair on wheels and shuts the door. I hop on for the ride.

At home, I leap to the kitchen table and nudge his snout with my head. He pushes me away to dig into his backpack. He takes out a plastic bag, opens it, and whiffs. I smelled it in the engine-car. It is pee from the female, in a soft white pouch. His nostrils flare and the edge of his mouth quivers, as if he is stalking a squirrel. He wrings the juice into a snap-lid dish and stacks it with others in the frosty box.

The sun is up when my eyes open. I stretch. Dad is still in the bed. This means he will not leave me for the day. Breakfast! I lick his eyelid. Breakfast!

"Yow!" He blinks at me.

We head to the kitchen. I weave in front of him, rubbing. Yes! Yes! Breakfast, Dad! Yes! His walking slows, and two times I get caught between his ankles. I am too excited to stop. "Watch it!" He catches himself against the wall. I rub again to make nice, to stay his good boy.

I feed on pork morsels in gravy. Dad feeds on a flat crunchy square with butter. He plays with his little talking box. "Hi, Sis. Me and Lickrish want you to come over for dinner."

That night Dad rolls Sis through the door. He brings a warm, fat chicken, and beer. They drink and chatter, happy as crows snitching French fries. I lick my lips and wait, a good boy. Sis cannot reach my bowl, so Dad fills it with tasty shreds of meat and gravy she saved on her plate. I gorge. Afterwards, Dad parks Sis near the couch, and they feed on frosty cream in front of the picture-screen. I curl on the lap of Sis and knead her small belly. She is softer than Dad. She strokes my chin when I tilt up my face. "Sweet Licorice, you have the most beautiful eyes."

She strokes down my back. "You need a girlfriend," Sis tells Dad.

"Me and Lickrish are fine."

"You have no social life."

"He's social enough." Dad shakes his head. "I have girlfriends."

"More than one? You mean for sex?" She leans toward Dad. "Who? PTs at the rehab?"

He hisses. "Nah, they're all . . . crazy."

"Not. I still have friends there."

Dad reaches over and scratches the spot above my tail. "They don't date Maintenance."

"Ever give it a try? You're good-looking—and sweet."

"You would say so."

"Yes, I would." Sis taps his forepaw and smiles. "Who then? I hear you're chummy with a cute brunette, a new patient."

"'Chummy?' I wish. She thinks I'm weird." He slugs from his beer. "Don't worry about me." He points to the rolling chair. "I'd just like to nail that mother-fucker! Too bad he's dead." His paw forms a knot.

"Do we still have to talk about that?"

"That fucking drunk! You'll never even know what sex feels like."

Sis kisses my head. "You think I was a virgin?"

"C'mon. You were the most innocent sixteen-year-old on the planet—now you're the most innocent twenty-four-year-old."

Sis looks down at me on her lap and cuddles my head. "I fantasize how it would feel with a man . . . like in romance novels. But what I don't know I can't miss, right?"

"Not right. You can't hide it from your twin."

"I just haven't found the right guy." She swats at his head. "You're the one that gets upset, Rick. Mom gives me a pill."

"Yeah, great." He scoops me up.

"Time to go home, Sis. Mom'll be waiting to get you ready for bed."

"Yep—and my Depends can only hold one beer."

"Funny." Dad says it with a tone that does not belong to the word. "Let me stick this guy in his crate and we can all get going."

The next night, we go to his Ami again. This time we stop, get out, walk, get back into the engine-car and roll some more. I want to go home to the bed. Dad crinkles a piece of paper and we stop again. My legs are tired from bracing in my cave.

Angry water grumbles in the distance. We walk. Salt mist is thick. We trot around a building, and Dad finds glass doors. He slides them open without using his tools. Inside is silence and dark. Dad puts on his coverings, opens my cave, and follows his light dot toward a room that smells female. There is no rabbit *pâté*!

I sprint next to Dad before he closes the door, but he does not see me. His light flows up the side of a bed. I want to pounce on the dot, but I have learned that it is really nothing, and Dad might not like me in the room. I stay back so he will not step on my tail.

Through the dark, I see a human on her back, eyes closed, short ginger fur on her head, cloth up to her neck. The light dot slides over the hump of her chest. It jumps to the bedside tray and finds a talking box. Dad picks up the box and sets it on a rolling chair nearby.

He climbs up the end of the bed, soft and quiet as a kitten, and loosens the sheet. He uncovers bare legs, slides off her pee pouch, pulls a plastic bag from his pocket, seals the pouch inside. He pushes his snout cover up and nuzzles into her underparts. The bed squeaks, and her eyes open. She gasps. I hop to the rolling chair to watch. Her arms flail toward Dad, but he is too far to reach. She yowls. Dad pounces.

Wow! Dad is a good pouncer for his size. He flattens across her forelegs and chest, cupping a front paw over her mouth, poking cloth into the opening. He squirms to pull long wraps from his pockets and ties her forelegs, one by one, to the bed rails.

Her chest and head jerk, but her belly and hind legs stay still. Dad moves back down. He licks without tiring, just like Mama when she scrubbed my underparts. I am lulled, knowing that Dad is taking good care of this female. But her eyes do not go calm. They dart from one side of the room to the other. Her forepaws yank at the wrappings. She does not like this kind of cleaning. Fear forms a cloud, but Dad does not smell it, and he cannot see the water of hurt from her eyes. He works hard, getting into her soft folds with his tongue, trying to make her fresh and tingly.

I hop to the side of the bed and creep toward her snout. I want to lap the water that runs down her chin, show her that cleaning is nice. I stop. Dad will see me, and I will not be his good boy.

He fixes his snout cover and climbs close to her face. Her head and forelegs go wild, like a butterfly under a paw. Dad covers her with his body. He pumps his haunches in soft movement and leaves his scent. He wipes her snout with his hand, like he does when he cleans my eyes. "I love you, beautiful," Dad whispers. She will not be lulled. I slink under the bed.

When he rolls the chair from the room, I run in front of it, happy to go. I leap into my cave and wait for him to take me.

At home in the kitchen he pulls out the pee pouch, like before. I sit on the table as he drains the pee into its dish. The smell brings her hurt close. I go to bed and curl up. I tongue a spot above my tail. The patch is not dirty but licking tingles and soothes me. I swallow fur and keep tonguing.

After that, I groom the spot whenever I am alone. The bare patch goes pink, and my prickly tongue rasps skin. I can taste my raw gravy.

On another night, I am lounging on the lap of Dad, and he is watching the picture-screen, eating Mac. I am full of duck *pâté* but waiting for my morsel of Mac. My scabby spot needs licking. I make a few quick swipes. Dad does not like when I touch it.

"What's the matter with you?" He tilts my face toward his snout and talks soft. "OCD kitty. What am I gonna do with you?"

I am not his good boy.

He plays with the buttons on the small gray box. "In Miami, a report of a man breaking into a house and raping a paraplegic woman in her twenties."

The belly of Dad knocks me to the floor. He sits straight.

"The victim is paralyzed from the waist down and says that she woke up while the intruder was performing oral sex. She was then raped and tied up. Her nurse found her this morning. According to Metro Police, there was no sign of forced entry. They strongly urge all women in the Miami area, especially those with disabilities, to keep their doors and windows locked. This is the second disabled woman to come forward this month. There are believed to be others. Police will not comment on whether they have a suspect."

The eyebrows of Dad pinch together. His mouth lets out air like when he is tired of me kneading his belly. The picture goes off. Time for the bed.

No. He goes to the kitchen, leaving a big chunk of Mac for me. I leap to it and pull it off the bun. Mac is salty and greasy, but I am not happy without Dad. I feed fast and go to the kitchen. Dad is taking his pee dishes from the heating box to the table. I hop next to them.

Some pees are light and some dark-yellow, faint scents and strong ones. Dad likes all kinds. He sits down and bends forward, stiff and focused, sucking in smells, like he is watching a bird he cannot reach.

My nose matches scents with the females I saw. I smell their fear and drop to groom the spot above my tail. The table wobbles and waves of pee spill over the dishes.

"Fuck!" Dad swats at me, and I dodge. I am off balance and hit my side on a chair on my way to the floor. I shake off the pain and leap to his lap to make nice, but land on a hard part I never felt before. Dad yowls and knocks me off. His face shows pain. I am bad! I hurt him. He hurt me. He hurt the female.

I go to the bed and squirm under it to groom. I cannot lull myself. I go to the kitchen to see if Dad will be nice. He is rubbing his lap to stop the pain. I slink back under the bed and lick.

The next morning, I stay hidden till I hear Dad in the kitchen. I go to my dish and feed on beef morsels and gravy. I am his good boy.

I hop to a chair to clean. I watch the butter on the plate in the middle of the table. Is it there for me? The talking box makes noise and Dad picks it up. I lean against it and hear Sis inside. "Have you read *The Herald*?"

"No."

I rub my snout on the box. I want Sis.

"Stop it." Dad pushes me away, but not hard. I go back and nuzzle.

"Are you listening? Lena got raped! My Cuban friend in rehab—a patient."

"Huh?"

"She's the first one with enough guts to tell the police. The story's in the paper."

"Was she hurt?"

"Yes! She was raped! . . . He had his mouth all over her."

Sis feels bad. I want to rub on Sis, but Dad blocks the talking box with his paw. "That's terrible."

"Lena said Marcia—from our same rehab—had an incident last month. Her wheelchair and phone were in the living room when she woke up in the morning, and her Depends was dry—like he changed her! She had taken a sleeping pill and didn't know what happened."

"I'm glad you're home with Mom."

"I bet there are other gals too embarrassed to call the police—I would be. Lena says they got DNA. And get this—her Depends was gone, probably a wet one!"

"Do they have a description of the guy?"

"I don't think so. It was probably too dark."

After that day, we are home many nights, cuddling in front of the picture-screen. Fur has grown in above my tail. I do not jump up on the table when Dad sniffs pee.

I have almost forgotten the hard walls of my cave till he pushes me inside. Sticking out all my legs only helps for a short time. I settle down and be his good boy.

We do not ride around long. We go inside and up many hard stairs. Dad stops at a flat space and sets down my cave. I want to wait here, but he does not know. He picks me up and climbs more stairs. He opens a door and sets me on carpet. I smell his hand covers and listen to the clink of his tools. There's a tap and a click and we are inside a dark room.

He opens my cave, but I do not move. I know what comes next. His light dot slips away. I do not want to see, but I cannot hold back. I race down the hall behind Dad and leap past him as the door closes. There she is, long brown fur spread over a white pillow. A rolling chair next to the bed. The light dot crosses the nightstand. No talking box. Dad works his way to her haunches and slides off the pee pouch. He bends to her underparts.

I am bad, so bad. I slink to the pillow and nuzzle her ear. Her eyes fly open. Her jaw moves, but no yowl comes out. Fear billows. Her paw moves under me, like she wants to rub my belly. I lean in. She pulls up a chain holding a tiny white box with a dark button. "Help! Help!"

She yowls. "Police! Po—"

Dad is up! His snout cover around his neck. He grabs the talking box and breaks it from the chain. There is a human inside, but it is not Sis. "Is this an emergency? State your passcode now if this is not an emergency."

Dad stares at the box. The female lets out another yowl.

Dad tosses the box and runs, slamming back the door and taking huge steps down the hall. I dash to my cave. Dad keeps going. No cave! Run with Dad! I dart ahead and wait for him to open doors. I sprint down the stairs. I run with Dad! Yes, yes! Happy, happy! I dash back and forth to catch his eye. Yes! We are out of there!

My neck is caught between his ankles.

I stop and shake off the pain. Dad dives headfirst, bumping downstairs, like I flop on the floor when it is good to see him, and I want my belly rubbed.

Yes! Yes! I will rub! I hop down. I nuzzle his cheek. Red meat shows near his ear, and his raw gravy is starting a puddle. I wait for Dad to shake off his pain. He closes his eyes. He wants me to leave him alone. I was bad.

He is asleep. The stairs are not soft like the bed, but we will stay here tonight. His lap is sideways, and there is no place to cuddle. I curl between his hind legs and rest my head, like the good boy I want to be.

A door above us squeaks open and one below. "Don't move," a man shouts. "You're under arrest." Heavy shoes clomp toward us. Bright lights.

Men are not all nice like Dad. We need to run. I lick his eyelid, but he will not blink. He stays still as a lizard when it is done playing.

Two men climb the stairs. I slip into shadow.

One man sits on his haunch and touches the neck of Dad. "So, this is the pervert—our urophiliac." He shakes his head and takes the front paw of Dad. "Barely a pulse. Concussion and maybe a broken back."

I slink down the stairs to wait for the outside door to open. I will come back in the morning, when the loud men are gone, and Dad and I are both hungry.

THE COLLECTED LETTERS
OF
LAWRENCE GILBERT
AND
GEORGE BURGHARDT

JACK MCCLELAND

undated

Larry—

Where the fuck were you?

—George

undated

George—

I'm around back.

—Larry

undated

Larry—

Just dropped by. See you at Chris's. Go Mad Dogs!!!

—George

undated

Larry—

The wrench is in your mailbox.

—George

undated

George—

I'm around back.

—Larry

undated

Larry—

Asshole. I came by to kick your ass. I saw you with "you know who." You lying fuck. I'm going to kill you.

—George

undated

George—

I'm around back.

—Larry

undated

Larry—

You were right about "you know who" that crazy bitch Karen. It's over. Headed for Chris's. Come on by and get drunk with me.

—George

P.S. Pay your fucking phone bill so I can call you.

P.P.S. Go Mad Dogs!!!

undated

Larry—

Here's the jumper cables. Put them around back inside the porch door. Thanks. See you at Chris's.

—George

undated

George—

Hope you see this. Couldn't wait. See you at Freddy's.

—Larry

undated

Larry—

Just dropped by to say one last goodbye. We're on our way. Karen says hello/goodbye to Judy. I'll call when we get settled.

—George

Feb. 5, 198-

Larry —

Fucking Florida. Eat shit Snowman. Karen's got a job. Already. I'm going to the beach. Think I'll lay around and get drunk and watch all the babes on the beach. Ha ha. Life is real tough here in tropical paradise. Tomorrow we look for a place to rent. Go Mad Dogs! Say hi to everyone at Chris's. Karen says hello to Judy. Oh gee, it's one o'clock already. Time for a pina colada!!!!!

—George "Floridaman" Burghardt

April 25, 198-

Mr. George "Floridaman" Burghardt—

Had this card laying around thought I'd send it. Mad Dogs Rule!!! Finally! We kicked their asses. Excuse the beer and puke stains. I'm writing this in Chris's. Weather sucks. Job sucks. Having fun. Wish you were here—and I was there. Judy says hello to Karen. Everybody here at Chris's says hi. Except Chris. He wants his twenty bucks.

—Larry

P.S. Don't get sunburned.

June 21, 198-

Larry—

"You know who" won't let me make any more long distance calls. So that's why the card. No job. Fuck it. Lying around on beach. Getting drunk. You should quit your job, dump Judy and come on down. We could party. Karen is coming home soon. Got to go.

—George

August 10, 198-

Larry—

Got a job. It sucks but only temporary. Hot as hell. Karen's coming up to see her parents etc. I can't get off so I'll just have to stay here and party while she's gone. Hello to all the assholes at Chris's. Sorry about you and Judy. Thanks for the call.

—George

December 21, 198-

George—

Merry Fucking Christmas. You probably won't get this in time but you know me. It's freezing here. You lucky bastard. I bet you're swimming right now. Laughing at us up here. Fuck you, George. Thinking of coming down to visit. Say hello to Karen for me. By the way—things are cool with Judy. We're friends.

—Larry

Feb. 19, 198-

Larry—

No phone. Karen moved out. Good riddance. Got arrested for Driving While Intoxicated. Bullshit. Nazi cops. Come on down. Lots of babes. Party time etc. etc.

—George

P.S. I have a spare sofa just waiting for you.

March 3, 198-

George

Get a phone. Still thinking of coming down to visit. Work sucks. Rained for a week. Judy said she saw Karen in town. Judy is going out with Freddy. What a pair. Everyone at Chris's says hey. Mad Dogs broke up. Oh well. It was getting boring anyway.

—Larry

P.S. Keep that sofa free.

June 12, 198-

Larry—

No job. No money. No house. No problems. Got fired. Assholes. Staying with this young babe Skye (that's really her name). Don't know how long. I'll be here so don't write. I'll send you a card when I get settled. Think about coming down. We'll party.

—George

August 3, 198-

Larry—

Hot as hell. Can't take it. Florida sucks big time. Tell you all
about it. Be back soon. I might be back before you get this.
Save a seat for me at Chris's.

—George

Feb 2, 198-

George—

Sorry about Karen and me. I should have told you in person but I couldn't. She's moving in. She's sorry too. These things happen. Let's be adults. Afterall we're all Mad Dogs. Right? Let's talk. Let's try and be friends. It's no one's fault. I feel real bad.

—Larry

undated

Larry—

I'm around back.

—George

MACHU PICCHU, 1999

LONNIE BYRDE

It was the end. Knew it from the moment I saw those filthy feet peeking beneath the sheets at me. How could any normal human being even *consider* crawling into bed with their feet that filthy? Maria's soles appeared to have actually been colored-in with black marker, then coated over with dust. The love of my life had, no doubt, completely lost her mind. Those disgusting feet were a billboard, announcing that Maria and I were not the same two people anymore. We most certainly weren't soulmates anyway.

Returning from a desert camping trip with some friends, Maria had begun walking everywhere without shoes, even outside. The girls had met a man on a donkey who sold them peyote. Maria swore this wasn't planned, but it didn't matter. My fiancée had warped, transformed from *Department Store Brand Hippy* into *Actual Hairy and High-All-The-Time Hippy*. She stopped shaving her armpits and legs. Her hair no longer knew the touch of a brush. She rarely even changed clothes anymore. And now she kept leaving her shoes at people's homes, just wandering away and forgetting them. Her peyote trip would last the rest of her life.

*

Three months later, I landed at Jorge Chávez International in Lima, Peru. I was met by an amiable, sausage-armed Peruvian driver. He held a cardboard sign containing my pen-scribbled last name. He led me to an orange, VW bug in a clay parking lot, then drove us upwards, into a winding road through high, brown hills. As a life-long Floridian accustomed to its swampy flatness, scenery of this kind lifted my spirits over the rainbow. What a miracle a mountain was! Scenery this detailed and natural only existed in storybooks and the movies.

Before long, the city of Lima lay below us as an immense carpet of clustered lights, nestled against an ice-blue ocean.

My driver patiently tolerated my chopped-up Spanish for what must've felt like an interrogation. I couldn't help myself though. Nothing charged my soul like traveling. I wanted to know everything. How was the nightlife in Lima? Were the girls beautiful? Was I safe?

My hostel was located in the Barranco section of Lima, a Catholic community under cliff walls lining the western coast. The hostel building was mustard-colored and clean with a friendly staff who spoke great English. I slept in a room with six bunk beds, yet my only roommates were a bushy-bearded Swiss backpacker and a Belgian photographer from New York, visiting his Peruvian fiancée.

As for myself, I was on a solo journey to Machu Picchu to celebrate the Turn of the Millennium. It was originally intended as a romantic bonding event with Maria, my live-in girlfriend. She was from Argentina, so going to South America just made sense. Also, visiting one of the Seven Wonders of the Modern World seemed like an exciting, relevant idea.

Machu Picchu was an ancient Incan village built with granite and limestone and etched into the Andes Mountains. It was a sacred religious site where the Incas performed human sacrifices, drinking and bathing in their blood. However, this year it would be the site of an all-night rave party with three DJ booths, and two-for-one light beers.

The event sprouted from a popular paranoia during this time that the world would end at midnight. A design flaw within the global computer matrix would self-destruct our planet with a rainstorm of nuclear rockets and failed airplanes, dropping everywhere like explosive death. Why not celebrate somewhere sacred? (Go ahead and eyeroll at the ignorance of the past, but back then who the hell really knew?)

The plan was to spend a few days in Lima, then fly to Cusco where we would take a train to Machu Picchu. Only, Maria and I had broken up. No, she left me. Wandered off from me as though I were another pair of her shoes. I tried to get a refund for the plane tickets but of course that was cosmically impossible. She still went but with a group of friends. I went alone.

*

Before everything in Peru went to Hell, I was doing fine, more or less, having fun, meeting people. Until the morning I went to retrieve my wallet from my locker. I opened the wallet and noticed right away something was off—it was empty. I peeled frantic through its folds. I pried my pockets repeatedly as though the contents might magically appear if I just kept looking for them. Everything was gone, except my ID, likely left behind as mercy for the pathetic *gringo* moronic enough to leave his wallet in his pants outside the room he slept in while visiting a third world country. I'd gone out that night drinking with my roommates but getting drunk too much and too often had caught up to me. Big time. This was a serious fuck up.

Predictably, having all of my money stolen changed my trip. It was Christmas Eve, a Thursday. All financial institutions, both North and South American, were closed until Monday. This meant that I was penniless (or, in this case, *sole*-less) for five entire days. Merry Christmas, loser!

I'd at least been smart enough to leave a credit card folded in underwear, but I'd never used the card before. When the bank saw a charge from South America, they pulled the plug instantly. Pleading, screaming, panicked phone calls got me nowhere. It was the holidays, and no one was particularly interested in my non-murder-related crisis. Even the US embassy was closed until Monday. The internet was in its embryonic phases in 1999 and nowhere near as useful as it would've been now. I was on my own.

I had a meeting with the manager of the hostel. Nice guy but what could he do except apologize? If I'd wanted security cameras or a trusty safe to put my valuables in, I should've paid for an actual hotel room. Sadly, my journalist salary, and need to find a new home when I got back, necessitated the cheap travel. I had no one else to blame.

After the meeting, I sat in the hostel's common area, sunk low into a sofa blooming with yellow upholstery foam. I thought over just what in the whole wide world was I going to fucking do. How was I going to *eat?* Sulking, I managed to find an American football game on the 70's-era TV, replete with rabbit-ear anntenae. The reception was dim and wobbly, but clear enough to watch. The sight of helmeted, padded men strategically assaulting one another soothed my nerves somehow. A comforting relic of home.

To my astonishment, a stocky, bald guy stepped in through the window on my right. I'd forgotten there were steps outside leading to that window, so this feat seemed miraculous of him. The guy looked late-twenties and wore a white tee with baggy, overlong surf shorts. He wore sandals. Behind him entered a tall, wiry man with tall, wiry hair.

The bald guy looked me over, this sad-faced white *puta* sitting there alone, dejected, watching American football. His name was Alberto. He introduced his taller friend as "Diego."

I told Alberto about my outlandish situation. I couldn't hold back. I even blurted a brief synopsis of my failed relationship, exactly like the miserable prick I was.

"Do not have worry," Alberto said. "I will take care of you. I will provide."

"How?"

"You have plane ticket to Cusco?"

"I do, yes."

"Diego and me, we will go with you. Take care of you there. Make sure you get to Machu Picchu."

"Why would you do that?"

"Because you need help, and we can give it, no? It is not fair what happened to you. I feel shame that a fellow Peruvian would do that to a visitor."

"Maybe I should just go back home somehow."

"Impossible, no. I will take care of you. It is okay. I will be your spiritual guide to Peru."

"You would do that? Just like that? You don't even know me."

"I do. I will. We will have fun. We will be good friends. Diego and I were not doing anything for the New Year anyway. We go together. We meet you there."

It was either hang with this *so-generous-it's-shady* guy or sleep on the streets of Peru. It was arranged, through my insistence, that he would take care of me until Monday when I could pay him back. Not a second longer. Alberto would only insist that he didn't want to talk about the money. He was more than happy to serve as the guide for my Peruvian journey. Meanwhile, he would feed and house me. He would take care of absolutely anything I needed. Money meant nothing.

What choice did I have?

*

The three of us entered a crowded, log cabin-style café with a fireplace. We sat at a varnished picnic table with candles and drank beer and ate soup.

"This is too much," I said, hollering to be heard over the din of yarn-hatted travelers. "You're too nice!"

"Stop your mouth! No such thing. You will have the time of your life. I guarantee, yes."

I asked Alberto to tell me his story. He was more than pleased to, naturally, exploiting that universal need we all have to explain ourselves. Alberto started his career in crime by dealing guns, a career which derailed when he got shot. The event happened in a hotel room where the client apologized profusely while Alberto stood there, clutching his left arm as his blood hosed itself over a shag-hair carpet. The bullet had made a mealy hole through his bicep, barely missing bone. Not feeling the pain yet, Alberto had simply repacked his weapons case with his one good hand and rode his motorcycle to the hospital.

Alberto stretched the collar of his shirt over his shoulder, showing me the scar, a two-inch divet, flesh-colored from healing.

He mentioned how that motorcycle was the same used to evade the police many, many times. Not that high-speed chases were common in his life, but certainly more common than mine. He never offered to tell me what the police were chasing him for, and I didn't ask. I only knew now that I was being involuntarily cared for by a South American criminal. Situation felt dicey enough as it was.

Alberto was about to continue with his story when he recalled me mentioning that I was a writer. He had the light-bulb idea for me to write a book about him. I would be his opportunity for immortality, manifested as some important literary figure. Launched by the powers of my biting insight, he would be made famous, larger than life, a legend, a parable of underdog turned top-dog.

I decided instead to call my parents and have them wire money to me, first chance I got. Only, that wasn't possible. I was too embarrassed. I would've rather slept on the streets, eating out of the garbage—anything but ask my family for money. Guess I was just raised that way. No, I much preferred hanging out with a potentially dangerous criminal. I could deal with this.

So I agreed emphatically with Alberto that I should write an epic work of literature about him. What a great idea, sure.

*

Before leaving the café, Alberto gave ecstasy pills to Diego and me. I took the pill just to be polite and because I had taken the drug over a dozen times with Maria, so I knew how harmless it was. Anyway, ecstasy was so named because it filled the user with an abundance of love and agreement. I felt like I could use something like that about now.

The drug seemed to hit Diego instantly as he then opened up to me. He was a former policeman who had gone AWOL. Joining the police in Peru was like joining the military. There was an oath of service involved, which meant you couldn't just walk off the job. However, Diego had just walked off the job. To him, the Peruvian Police were becoming more about causing conflict than preventing it. Also, they frowned on their officers using drugs, which became an unacceptable policy for him. Alberto, his friend since childhood, who had chosen lawlessness over the law, now paid for anything Diego needed, same as me.

The three of us walked around Barranco that night, making our way towards the town's *zacolo*. This was what they called any main square. The focal point was always either a monolithic stone water fountain or a Gothic, two-tiered Catholic church. Sometimes both.

128

Wherever we went, I noticed how my new companions made sure to keep me between them.

"Are you guys protecting me?" I asked Alberto. "Am I in danger?"

"*Claro...,*" he said. *Of course.* He explained how it wasn't wise for a foreigner to wander Lima by themselves, especially after dark

A silhouetted group of young men passed us. One of them whistled, a two-note tweet. Alberto and Diego both repeated the whistle back at him. I'd come to learn this was Peruvian youth shorthand for: *"I see you. I know you. We're good."*

Absolutely *everyone* knew Alberto. We could duck into the most random *bodega* imaginable, and the shopkeeper would know him. So would the customers. He was particularly popular with women. I wasn't sure whether any of this was from him being beloved or feared. I tried not to worry about it. I would find out soon enough.

*

Alberto brought me to the Lima cliffs and the ecstasy kicked in. Warmth and wonder lathered me as, beneath my feet, a distant, crashing surf appeared as a foamy fringe to an infinite, black blanket of ocean. I bounced my knees, as though preparing to jump, enjoying how this made my new friends nervous. I had no intention of ever ending my life on purpose, but I relished their concerned yelps. That someone cared.

Walking me back through downtown, back to my hostel, Alberto asked me if I'd ever smuggled cocaine before. I confessed the thought had not once crossed my mind ever.

"You like to make money?" he asked me.

"Legally, yes."

"Because I could use a connection in the US. Think you could help me get a visa?"

"I have no control over that. I'm sorry."

"But maybe you could do something. You're American. I am banned from America. I go to try, I am arrested,"

"I'll see what I can do," I said, just to put a halt to his requests. There was absolutely nothing I could do to help him re-enter a country from which he was barred, not even my own country. *Especially* my own.

I spent the next couple of days still trying to get my hands on some money. The owner of the hostel was nice enough to drive me to the one bank open in Lima. He served as interpreter between the bankers and me. But no one could help. There was no way to get my hands on my money, except through a bank transfer, which wasn't possible until Monday.

I called my credit card company. I called my bank in Miami. I emailed CEO's. I emailed everyone. No one was interested.

*

Alberto, Diego, and I each flew to Cusco on separate flights because I'd already bought my own ticket the day before being robbed. Their afternoon flights were simply the next two available.

I landed at Cusco Airport, which was small enough that I could watch Alberto's plane land and even de-board. I met him at his arrival gate, but he wasn't alone. He'd met a petite, raven-haired, Middle Eastern girl during his flight. They couldn't take their eyes off each other.

"Why do you keep looking at me?" he asked her.

She smiled and shrugged. He asked her what she kept looking at five more times and received the same response. I took a seat on the floor and went back to my book (which I'd stolen from the hostel.) I intended this as a chance for the two of them to have some privacy. Instead, they took a seat on the floor right next to me. He continued asking her what she was looking at, and she kept smiling and giggling. Drove me nuts.

Alberto held an undeniable power over women, and I was jealous. While he never lacked for female companionship, I suffered endless heartache. Truth was, dirty feet or clean, I was traumatized by my relationship with Maria ending. The way she had become so hostile towards me, her respect for me all but evaporated. At times,

130

it seemed maybe she even hated me. She was sick of being poor. Disgusted. I had let her down as a man.

I was a broke and moody man-child, self-involved, and badly in need of a haircut. Not wishful ingredients in a soulmate, I was sure. In hindsight, I didn't understand what had taken her so long to leave me. She must've genuinely loved me at some point.

We were in Peru at the same time and never once saw each other. Good for her.

*

We stayed at Alberto's cousin's hostel, which overlooked all of Cusco and its high-walled roadways. The town formed a clustered and erratic stone maze against the lush countryside.

We spent our Christmas holidays in coffee shops, high out of our minds, but using our expanded consciousness as a bridge for meeting new people. There was an unspoken bond between all of us foreigners that were here for the New Millennium. Though traveling from different parts of the world, we now shared the same geography, the same oxygen, the same events. The same frantic need for dancing, fun, love, for any stimulation at all practically.

That first Monday after Christmas, I finally had the money wired and I was able to re-pay Alberto. He wouldn't take the money directly, so I returned his favor by paying his and Diego's meals and drinks wherever we went. The amount of money I'd transferred still was too conservative though and in no time at all I was low on funds again. I eventually needed Alberto to take over helping me out agaim. He treasured this since it meant I pretty much belonged to him now. My duty in return was to hang out with him, observe him and his life, and later write a book about him. He was excited.

*

One morning, the three of us had breakfast together on the hostel's patio, which always gave us a far-reaching view of the entire town below. Alberto told me he'd learned that the rave at Machu Picchu was cancelled—relocated to a village in the mountains of *Ollantaytambo*.

He seemed unfazed by this news. Alberto existed in a fairly steady state of all-encompassing happiness. He was always, always smiling. I had to ask him about it. Why was he in such a damn good mood all the time?

"Because my mind is healthy," he answered. "My body too. My mental state is peaceful. Whenever I am hurt or face some problem, I look at it from a wider way. That helps reduce my anxiety."

"I wish I could be more like you." I didn't know where those words came from, but I said them.

Alberto took a joint from Diego. He spoke between puffs: "I consider every soul as human being. Basically we are all the same. Nothing different. Physically we are the same. If you ask scientists what are the differences in the brain or in the neuron...nothing. We are emotionally same, mentally also same. I never look at human beings as president or policeman, king or criminal. Whenever I meet new people, I say, 'Look at them. They are just other human beings...my brother or sister.' That is all."

Spiritual guide indeed.

*

On New Year's Eve, we took a train first to the town of *Aguas Calliente* where we next grabbed a taxi. Alberto sat in the front seat and I sat in the back with Diego. We rode through the hills as the sky turned purple, tapered in stars. The countryside became dotted with orange lights and I asked about them.

"Those are people burning piles of their clothes," Alberto told me. "It is a New Year's tradition in Peru."

"Like they're shedding their skin?"

"Yes, so you understand?"

"I understand."

We rode on. Alberto, under the influence of more ecstasy, chatted non-stop. I did my best to pay attention, but my attention kept getting caught by the bonfires of clothing we kept passing. Darkened figures crowded each glow, an array of orange, watching faces hovering just above the flames.

In a couple of hours, we reached the location of the rave, a lit-up square of land surrounded on every side by mountains. While waiting in line to get in, enveloped in darkness, the ecstasy hit me right as the New Year countdown started. Was this it? Was this the actual end of the world? My nerves buzzed. It was the apocalypse! I felt scared. It was so completely dark, and I was utterly alone. Immersed in strangers. How the hell did I end up here? I was just a small town kid from North Florida. My parents were even still married. The count was down to three seconds already. Two. One. Then…nothing. The music stopped. There was a collective gasp just before partiers let loose with a long chorus of shrieks and cheers. Anyone within arm's length of each other reached out and embraced, tight as if having survived some treachery. People kept hugging. Strangers, lovers, friends, everyone. We were alive. Everything was okay. Put that music back on.

*

We stayed up dancing the entire night. By morning we lay buried in a living carpet of bodies, most of them female, all of us on ecstasy. We huddled more for warmth than anything sexual, many wearing jackets beneath layers of blankets. That mountain frost had a strong sting, and the drugs made every sensation multiplied.

We caught a bus back to *Aguas Callientes*. There, Alberto said he would see me back in Cusco. He had some business to attend to. Diego would go with him, of course. I thanked Alberto from the bottom of my heart. He'd done it—he had gotten me to the rave. I'd actually made it, despite getting robbed. I would also finally see Machu Picchu now. It was my original purpose for coming and I wasn't even sure why I was going there anymore.

I checked into a hostel Alberto had paid for and I slept until the next day, awakening only once to the drumming of a hard rain against my window. The next morning I took a tourist bus to the holy site where Incas once lived. There, I found stone ruins arranged on curvy, parallel terraces, long and narrow, like shelves engraved along the mountainside.

From what I understood, most of these stone buildings were homes but others were ceremonial. The place felt shimmer-level sacred. The idea that an all-night rave would ever have been held here felt farcical and obviously never true to begin with. There were well-funded organizations to prevent such madness.

I made a seat for myself on a stone ledge and drank in the terrain, marveling at all that jutting earth, that jungly covering, spreading far into the horizon. A milky, gray fog filled the valleys and I understood that if I could make it to a place like this, then I could literally do anything I wanted. I felt a power I hadn't felt in probably never. My fate was in my own hands and always had been, even at my lowest. *Look at where the fuck I am. Look at me! King of the Universe!*

Not sure if it was the energy of a 15th century Inca citadel rubbing its shine on me, but I took off my shoes. I dug my naked feet into the soft ground, deep as I could push them, deep into that ancient soil. I wiggled my toes and they squished, becoming filthy.

*

Alberto tried getting my assistance with smuggling drugs to the US repeatedly. I declined. After moving to New York later that year, I got an email from him, pleading for money. He was in a bad situation. But I couldn't help him. I simply couldn't. Not just then. The deposits and broker fee for my new downtown Manhattan apartment had left my bank account decimated. I felt terrible.

I also never wrote a book about him.

It was at the entrance of Jorge Chávez International, mere minutes before my departure, where Alberto confessed he and Diego had been the ones to pilfer the contents of my wallet from my locker. It was my own money the three of us had been having fun with. They were the thieves.

Diego appeared sheepish, but amused. Alberto seemed apologetic, but also as if I must have known all along. I hadn't though. I was genuinely shocked. Not for one second had I thought of this.

I laughed and my two Peruvian companions laughed with me. We let the laughter go on for a while. It was just so funny that he'd even bothered telling me.

"That's awesome," I said. Because how pitiful would this trip have been otherwise?

I hugged them good-bye. For the fifth time. I almost couldn't stop. I hefted my backpack over my shoulder, lifted my duffel. I darted off and went searching for my airplane.

BONOBOS

JANET BOHAC

It had been going on for a while, as these things sometimes did. I'm not going to pretend I don't remember how it started, but you just have to understand: kitchens are strange places filled with strange people. We didn't always follow the rules others took for granted. We were not polite. We didn't mollify like the servers who faced the public and worked for tips. We could be crude, sometimes criminal. If I'd had a nickel for every cook I worked with over the last twenty-something years who had a record, I could buy Starbucks. Not the whole shebang, but definitely a fucking Frappacino or two.

Back before it even started, there were things like Chef telling the dish dog, Aaron, that he wanted to get between the dish dog's mom and ex-girlfriend.

"Like an Oreo? Like a chef sandwich and you're the creamy center?" I tossed this out just to see if I could get him going while I chopped some romaine for the Caesar salads.

"Oh, there'll be cream, all right!" Chef exclaimed. He made his standard hip action and held out his hands. We were given to understand that, in his mind, his penis was the size of a telephone pole.

Aaron rolled his eyes and went back to his dish pit. You'd think after a year he would've been inured to this, but no. He still got his feelings hurt when the cooks talked about fucking his mom, Katie, who was eighteen when she had him, who was petite and tended the bar and had just gotten a boob job paid for by I don't even know who. (I walked in on her in the restroom with another server feeling her implants. When she asked if I wanted to feel them too, I said, "Naw, I'm good," which was pretty much my standard line to any such invitations that happened at work.) Maybe it was the details the cooks indulged in, the scenarios they made more elaborate than the situation called for, or the fact that Aaron did not get along with his mom especially well. She had kicked him out of the apartment as soon as he graduated high school and moved her most-recent still-married boyfriend in. Aaron had to endure a lot of *"That's not what your momma said last night"* comments, as well as a staggering number of *"Are you my new daddy?"* jokes.

There was the time I requested a night off on the calendar and Chef's three-year-old in her older brother's Cat Boy costume scribbled over it. He didn't realize until the next week what had happened and made a half-assed apology. This was the same week the eldest kid's bunny died. I gave him a long, pointed stare. "It's okay," I said, pretending it wasn't. "But next time, the dog gets it." The other cooks howled and for the next week my nickname in the kitchen was "Bunny Killah" instead of the usual "Mad Dawg."

Nobody else but me heard it when Chef brushed past me and said, "Leave my dog out of it, but could you kill my wife, please?"

I replied, "Sure," with the swiftness and nonchalance of a real Bunny Killah. I think he might've even been alarmed I meant it.

So when he said something about me giving him a pair of my dirty underwear as I was cutting carrots at my station, I said, "Silly wabbit. That's how you get caught. You give me a pair of her clean underwear and I give 'em back to you dirty."

The look he gave me was priceless. I think he was impressed with my on-the-fly ingenuity, but that's what line cooks did: a gluten-free vegan walked into a steakhouse and you had to tunnel through the coolers for presentable zucchini, tomatoes, and eggplant to *sauté* in garlic and olive oil to put atop some quinoa and white beans. A *filet mignon* came back that was supposed to be a well-done veal porterhouse because the server was a certifiable idiot and you stole it from the next ticket and sent it out like it was all magic.

So when he stuffed the blue Victoria's Secret thong in the pocket of my chef coat one night, I guessed he was serious.

By this time we'd worked together for several years and we had an inexplicable ESP going on. I could finish his sentences and often did. We shared the same inability to speak when things started jamming in the kitchen, but we wordlessly handed each other utensils and pans and a pinch of garlic at the right time like one organism. I might have plating up a ten-top across the pass from him, handing dishes to servers, piping whipped cream onto a profiterole, and notice him interrupted by a server's FAQ and forgetting an ingredient in the scampi. "Capers," I might have said. Or "thyme," when I saw that rare blank look on his face. I was like a jumpstart to his brain or an external hard drive.

I waited that first time. I had the thong in a baggie (sealed for freshness!) and hung onto it until the inevitable happened: his wife came into the kitchen, reamed him a new one and cut off his balls for good measure with the serrated edge of her voice. Something about how a guest didn't like how the calamari was prepared and it tasted like rubber bands and she'd had to comp that part of the ticket. She routinely did this whenever she got stressed out and seemed to enjoy doing it in front of his staff. I couldn't imagine a sex life with this woman after a scolding like that, and yet the scoldings happened on a weekly basis. The sex, we were all given to understand, had not happened since the third kid—she of the Cat Boy suit—had been conceived and his wife now insisted he get a vasectomy. He usually just turned back to the char-broiler or fiddled with the Pandora station or disappeared to the upstairs office as soon as the dinner rush was over.

I stuffed the baggie into his chef coat pocket when the other cooks went out for a smoke break. "Knock yourself out."

He met my eyes for a second longer than usual, but I heard the "thank you" no one but me could hear. We guessed we were really doing this.

Cooks came and went. Artie was there for about six months, then left in a huff in the middle of a dinner rush when there was disagreement about how many baby lobster tails to float in a bowl of seafood bisque. He kept putting several on top with the *crème frache* instead of the one (for a cup) or two (for a bowl) and after about the fourth time, Chef's fingers scooped into the bowl and expertly flicked the extra tails out onto the stainless steel of the pass.

"Two!" he bellowed. He was matter-of-fact, not mean, but he'd had enough, and baby lobster tails were cutting into his profit.

Next thing we knew, Artie was gone and never came back. He threw his white apron in the trash on his way out and must have called his mother or the Harbor Transit bus to pick him up, because Artie didn't drive.

The next cook, Tim, who also didn't drive, was a petite, even-tempered guy who liked to get high and play online video games with kids half his age. And fish. When he texted for the third time that he wanted to go fishing instead of working his shift, Chef texted him, *No*, and Tim texted, *Fuck you*, and that was the last we saw of Tim until his mugshot showed up in the local news. He pleaded to walking into a stranger's house and exposing himself to a sixteen-year-old, but if that was the plea bargain, he was probably having sex with an underage kid he'd met gaming online when her parents walked in. I guess we'll never know. I sometimes imagine Tim in jail, unable to play video games, get high, or fish, and I shake my head. What gets into people?

There was Steve who made the news, too, by propositioning an Uber driver. Steve didn't drive either. Chef fired him when Steve threatened to punch the hostess, who was fresh out of high school, in the throat. There was Patrick who tried to get hugs from the servers and was on the sex offenders' registry. He didn't last long because he kept asking the staff for money and rides home. Eton lasted a while, then quit in a kerfuffle when he got switched from salary to hourly and took it as a slight to his ego.

Then came Vichy. No one else called him that but me and only to myself. At least Vichy could drive himself to work, work the line, and take direction. He'd been a chef in his own kitchens at the local yacht clubs. I sometimes couldn't tell if his clowning was an act to disarm Chef or if he was really that goofy. Things he said just didn't add up and there were times, like when Chef went to pick up his kids from school, that Vichy's act slipped and a much more steely person peeked through for a moment. He clearly had issues, like Asperger's or autism, and I think when he first arrived he had designs on Chef's job until he realized the only reason chef had his job was because his in-laws bought the restaurant for him when he knocked up their daughter.

It was all a wealth redistribution scheme, and Chef wasn't going anywhere.

That's when I felt Vichy's attention focus on me.

"Why don't you jump on the line?" he asked me one day when Chef was out.

"It's Chef's kitchen. He can put me wherever he wants," I said. Why would I want that?

It was thirty degrees hotter on the line, a ball-breaking pace, with Chef hovering over every move. No, I had the sweet spot, making salads and appetizers, prepping and expo-ing and finishing desserts.

Vichy told me stories about his last kitchen, a position I had interviewed for. I'd quickly shut down the interview when the owner's first question was, "Are you married?"

"Seriously?" I asked.

"Seriously."

"I've never had anyone ask me that. It's actually illegal for you to ask me that." I slid my resume across the table.

"Well, if it's illegal, then I've been illegal for forty-five years!" He laughed in a vain attempt to disarm.

I sat looking at him and he got uncomfortable and defensive and told me how many successful businesses he had run while I calmly stared at him and just wanted to leave. When I got home, I emailed him the EEOC's guidelines about what questions may not be asked by prospective employers. I never got a reply, but then, I wasn't expecting one.

So Vichy had worked for that guy for three years, then was fired via text while on vacation, probably because the dickwad didn't like paying Vichy $60K plus benefits. Now in his fifties, Vichy was going to have to be just another line cook at half the price unless he could find a kitchen of his own. He told me he'd heard from his *sous chef* that the dickwad's manager, Rayna, had offered the *sous chef* a blow job in the walk-in cooler his first day of work. He sounded a bit miffed in retrospect that he had never been offered the same.

"Ah. The kitchen blow job." I'd heard of such things before, of course, but never felt the need to be a party to them. I was a line cook, a damn good one, and didn't need to show my submission to any fucking *sous chef*. In my best *nothing to see here, folks* voice, I said and shrugged, "Well, we don't have a walk-in here, so . . . "

Vichy tried other avenues, trying to suss out my weakness. He'd lived in Alaska for fifteen years. Did I want to run away to Alaska and climb Denali with him?

"Naw, I'm good," I said.

Didn't I want my own kitchen?

"Naw, I'm good."

I felt him searching, rooting around for the thing that bound Chef to me and me to Chef and the truth was simpler than he ever could have imagined: Chef treated me well. He gave me the days off I asked for (with that one bunny-killing exception). He gave me the wages I asked for. He gave me the kitchen spots I liked. He came when I called because my car died in the winter. He helped me out when my landlady asked all sorts of crazy questions before she would rent to me. I owed him for everything that was good in my life. I came in on short notice and took the night off when we had no reservations. I cut the carrots the way he wanted, stocked the coolers the way he asked, washed the dishes when yet another dish dog crashed and burned. But Vichy wanted to find something he could take to the wife or the in-laws. He wanted to see if there was any way to get to that top position short of knocking up the wife.

Meanwhile we celebrated Chef's fortieth birthday. The wife gave him a pair of work shoes which seemed especially cheap of her, considering it was a business expense they could write off. She also gave him a hickey on his neck about which he was openly ashamed. There was no flaunting that on the line. No jokes, no mention of it. None of us could figure out why he reacted the way he did, pulling his collar to cover it, hunching over the char-broiler like he wanted to just slide through the grates. I thought maybe it was a bridge too far—being branded by her when she controlled so many other aspects of his life. She had meant for people to see it. She said it was a joke. He wasn't laughing and we wouldn't laugh about it either, if we knew what was good for us.

On the nights she worked the front of the house, he continued to make her dinners, a salad with whitefish or *tournedos* with Bernaise sauce, maybe, or a *filet mignon* with mushroom *demi-glace*. They bought a bigger house so the kids could each have a bedroom as they grew older. He worked every night except Sundays when the kitchen was closed, and they went to church with the in-laws, and Thursdays were their official date night. They went to couples counseling. He got his wisdom teeth pulled. She got Bell's Palsy and half of her face drooped.

When he handed me thong panties, I thought it was the least I could do, and gave it back to him the next day, and we never spoke about it.

Vichy finally left when a chophouse opened in the village and I was glad to see him go. Now I don't even remember his real name.

ROCKY MEMORIES

SIDNEY J. DRAGON

Our world today has come a long way but, back then, a guy ran the serious risk of getting his butt kicked if he wore anything fruity. It was brave of these people to cross-dress for the evening. Many of them around me wore what's now called "cosplay." They were there for a weekly screening of *The Rocky Horror Picture Show*. It was my first time. My best friend Rachel had invited me to the seventh anniversary show at the Sena Mall Movie Theater in a suburb of New Orleans.

The film started and, to my amazement, the roar of the audience was like a sporting event. Shouts and catcalls occasionally drowned the film out. People hurled comments at the screen, often in answer to something one of the characters had said or would say. These moviegoers broke every rule of proper theater etiquette imaginable: no shouting during the movie, or getting out of your seat, or throwing food, lighting lighters, or just being generally unruly. They were given a pass to act like crazy people!

When the castle caretaker and disguised space alien, Riff Raff, appeared in the tower window for his solo in "Over at the Frankenstein Place," the theater crowd went berserk. They held lighters and swayed to the song. My friend Rachel told me the actor who played Riff Raff also wrote the music, lyrics, and the original play. I fell in love with Richard O'Brien right there. He lived the writer's dream! Just that thought alone was powerful enough to keep me coming back. I spent the rest of the film in awe, even nervously joining in some of the callbacks.

The film's plot involved Brad and Janet, a newly engaged couple whose car breaks down in a rainstorm. They leave the car and stumble upon a castle, hoping to use their phone to call for help. The castle is occupied by beings in strange costumes who are there to celebrate an annual meeting of sorts. Brad and Janet then meet Dr. Frank N. Furter, the castle's owner, a scientist vampire alien who likes to wear women's clothing. His newest lab creation is a golden-briefed beefcake named Rocky whom he lusts after. As the movie continues, Brad and Janet are both seduced by Frank N. Furter and others. The poor couple never get to use the phone.

After that night, I was a Rocky whore. As long as my grades didn't suffer, I'd decided I deserved some weekend fun, and part of that fun would be *Rocky Horror*.

In the summer 1986, I befriended several "cast members" who performed in front of the screen for the floor show. One night, I got up the nerve to perform Riff's part where he sang alone in the castle tower. I'd cobbled together a makeshift, hunchback Riff Raff costume from thrift store finds. I soon became an accepted part of the group.

Cast members came and went, sometimes after only one show. I personally found my biggest problem was falling in love with every actress who played Magenta. This character was the Goth maid of the castle who shared an incestual relationship with Riff Raff, her brother. I tended to get schoolboy crushes on my fellow performers and occasionally ended up sleeping with some. Young hormones ruled the day, even in Rocky's world.

By the winter of 1987, I was more heavily involved with this movie than ever, but my personal life was changing. I accepted a job on the Walt Disney World College program for the following Spring term and had to leave New Orleans for three months. Walking out of the theater that last night was one of the most difficult things I ever had to do. For me, it was rarely the actual performance of the show that held the attraction—though there *was* a naughty thrill which came from singing and dancing before an audience while wearing bikini briefs and a gold lamé tunic—the real rush came from the people I'd met and acted with. (I don't miss the movie so much. I can watch it on home media whenever I want now, but I do miss the people.)

Those months at Disney were the longest of my life. I was somewhat envied by my roommates in Florida, as I often got a good bit of mail from my Rocky friends. I felt like Dorothy in *The Wizard of Oz*. I kept telling people I wanted to go home. I missed New Orleans too much. I was depressed and wrote my Rocky friends almost constantly, as if needing to ease the pain of a long distance break-up. My roomies thought I was nuts.

SIDNEY DRAGON

Finally, my three month sentence was up, and I went home. I even left Florida two days early so I could make it to the Friday night *Rocky Horror* performance and surprise everyone. I was downright trembling when my former carpool friends drove into the Sena Mall parking lot.

I became swamped with people wanting to hug or kiss me. It was a feeling never duplicated, and I've looked everywhere. Although I was informed my part was recast, I knew it was only a matter of time before I would slip back into the garter again.

*

The summer of 1988 was one of further growth and change for me. I moved out on my own, fell in love several times, and really came into my own as a young adult. That August was the tenth anniversary of *Rocky Horror* at the Sena Mall. A huge party was planned, and my cast was to perform the Saturday night show. We only had one problem: our Frank N. Furter had skipped town. Luckily, Larry Von Ritzmann stepped in. He was a talented local actor, very generous in his performance and theatrical knowledge. Larry took over directing the show, teaching us a lot about acting and professionalism.

He retooled our show while making us still want to bring something new and give our all to every performance. We became the Scene One Players with the slogan: "If you've seen one player, you've seen 'em all!" Larry wasn't always the easiest director to work with, but you still knew his notes were best for the show. I'll never forget his advice for stage acting vs. film or television: "Reach up and scratch the elephant's ass because you have to reach way up!" In other words, it was important to make our movements big enough to reach the very back of the theater.

After Halloween, Larry dropped *Rocky Horror* in hopes of starting a local repertory company. Sadly, that fell through due to a lack of funding. I stayed in touch with Larry on and off until he passed away in '95.

Early '89, I again heard the call of *Rocky Horror*. It was a very emotional time as the good old Sena Mall was closing its doors

151

forever. At first, we couldn't believe it. It was like we were being forced to leave our home.

Many of the cast members from past years came for this final show. It was a homecoming, of sorts.

Cast and audience shed tears. I'll never forget that night. I looked out over the sold-out theater during the song "Over at the Frankenstein Place," and couldn't see the movie on the screen for all of the lighters that were lit and swaying.

After the show I stood in the lobby, saying goodbye to my best friends. Larry approached me in full Frank N. Furter make-up but paired with a tuxedo. He hugged me like the older brother I felt he was. He also made sure he was the last to leave the building. Larry said he was the first in when Rocky opened and now he was the last person to leave when it closed. I noticed a glistening in his eye. We shook hands and hugged again, then he left. I was alone but for the two friends I was riding home with. We stood in the dimly-lit parking lot. We watched as the Sena Mall sign went dark for the last time and my own tears finally came.

The Rocky Horror Picture Show moved to another theater and my cast moved with it. We had our in-house squabbles, our politics, our romances, but it never felt the same. The theater was smaller, more cramped.

That last night at the Sena Mall though, as my cast members linked arms around a bowling alley pool table, we sang the reprise for "Science Fiction, Double Feature" and understood how a magical chapter in our lives had been closed.

MRS. PUTNAM'S PLACE

JESSICA OESTERLE

Ruth Putnam spent most days fishing the back creek or tending the vegetable garden she'd once tilled with her husband. She spent most evenings rocking on her porch with a glass of whiskey. She knew Robert wouldn't have approved of her drinking, but, she decided, he wasn't around to stop her.

Ruth was leaning against the kitchen sink and planning the day ahead, when her phone rang on the counter beside her. She saw her daughter's name glowing on the screen and scooped it up.

"You should really get someone to help you, Mom," Lena told her over the phone. "You're not as young as you used to be."

Ruth moved the phone to her other ear. "I'll be careful. Just takes me a little longer these days."

"I'm sending the Robinsons' boy over. You shouldn't do it by yourself anymore."

"I don't need some teenager here bothering me," Ruth fumed. "Stop sticking your nose in."

"Mom."

"Just like your father. Telling me what to do and when. I'm capable of taking care of myself, thank you very much. Been doing it longer than you."

Ruth hung up. She snatched her gardening gloves and pushed through the screen door, letting it slam behind her. Across the yard, she unlocked the shed and swung open the door, hinges whining. Ruth yanked the canvas cover off of the rototiller, flinging dust and dead bugs into the air. The shed was small, and she loathed enclosed spaces. Not enough air to breathe. Her chest tightened. Ruth hurried to extract the rototiller and it rolled out of the shed easily. After gassing it up, she put her weight on the handle and lifted the machine onto its back wheels.

"Some stranger in my garden," she muttered. She rolled the rototiller through the yard.

Reaching the spring green over the septic tank, Ruth thought of the first time Lena had brought her husband home. It had been the

Easter right after they'd gotten engaged. Their septic tank had dropped dead a few weeks prior, but Ruth was so excited to see them, she'd neglected to mention it over the phone. An empty pit yawned in the front yard where Robert and his buddies had hauled out the old, busted tank. He was still waiting for the new one to arrive, but, in the meantime, they'd parked a Port-O-Potty nearby. It was a monument to their poverty, and Ruth could tell Lena had been humiliated. That turned out to be the last Easter they had with Robert.

The mid-April sun now fell on Ruth's face, and the scent of wet soil filled her lungs. The lawn was reviving around the garden edges. Wouldn't be long before she was weeding, stopping nature from reclaiming her little patch of nowhere. She smiled in peaceful gratitude before pulling on her gloves.

"Mrs. Putnam?"

"Oh!" she started.

The Robinsons' boy stood there, lanky and disheveled, hands shoved deep inside his pockets. "Name's Brett. Thought I'd come and see if you needed any help with that rototiller? Your daughter sent me."

Ruth waved a dismissive hand and pushed the rototiller through the garden gate. She shut it behind her. "What's she paying you?"

"Oh, uh." Brett looked uncomfortable. This amused Ruth, who knew this teenage specimen would never have bothered with her without payment. "Well," he began.

"I don't like people in my garden, Brett Robinson," she cut in. "Nothing personal. How about I make you a deal?"

"Ma'am?"

"You take my daughter's money, and you go do whatever you do." Ruth propped an elbow atop the rototiller. "And I'll tell Lena that you were real helpful. It'll be our secret."

"I don't know."

"Sure ya do. You seem like a nice kid. You can even stop by later to ease your conscience." She offered a sweet smile, formerly her stock and trade. Ruth was relieved she still remembered how to barter with it.

"Well," he said, "guess there's no harm."

"Atta boy," Ruth said. "See ya around."

Ruth reached for the ignition and turned it over. The rototiller burped itself to life, its metal blades chewed into the ground and exposed the raw, dark soil below. It pulled itself down the garden, leaving behind plush rows of earth in its wake.

She was relieved the Robinson boy had accepted the deal. She'd gotten along well enough without a man to run her life. *What is the use of them, anyways?* Ruth thought to herself. *Always getting what they want through bullying.* Her mind returned to Robert. Most everyone had backed off when Robert got mad, especially Ruth whose quiet manner he mistook for weakness. Over the years, she'd grown accustomed to his outbursts, and spent more and more time on gardening, canning, baking, and not asking Robert where he'd been all night. Looking back, she barely recognized the wife, the person, she'd been ten years ago. Ruth had spent enough time beholden to her husband's whims. Now, she decided, she would indulge her own.

*

Today was a good day, Ruth thought as she rocked on her porch. The sun, low on the horizon, cast a warm glow over her face and work clothes. She hadn't bothered to change or clean the dirt from under her fingernails. Instead, she'd poured a drink and retired to the old rocking chair. A pair of barn cats sunned themselves on the porch steps nearby, waiting for dinner.

"Mrs. Putnam?"

"Hi there, Brett," she said, not looking up.

He shifted his weight and hitched up a plastic bag. "Looks like you got the whole garden done today."

Ruth raised her eyes and leaned back in the rocker. "What ya got there?"

"It's a present. My mom thought you might like some of her sourdough. She's been baking like crazy since she got laid off. We can't eat it fast enough."

"That's very kind." Ruth pushed herself onto her feet. She hadn't heard that Mrs. Robinson lost her job, but she wasn't surprised. Ruth had lost her own shifts at Ace Hardware, a few weeks into lockdown. At least she could collect social security. "You wanna come in? I have a few jars I canned last fall. I've been meaning to send them over."

"I don't think—"

"Not at all." Ruth motioned to him with her glass. She opened the screen door with her free hand.

He followed her into the kitchen. He stood awkwardly while she scrubbed her fingernails clean in the sink. She lifted the loaf out of its bag, then brought the bread to her nose, savoring its yeasty tang. "Your mother is good," Ruth said. "It's hard to get it crusty like this."

"I guess," Brett said. "You shoulda seen the first few ones."

Ruth laughed. She remembered her first attempts at baking bread. She'd been pregnant with Lena and newly married. It was her time to make the perfect life, the one her mother had never made for her. There would be a vegetable garden and venison jerky and fresh baked bread every day, with a father to coach little league and to love. There would be love.

"It's just down in the cellar," Ruth said, placing the loaf on her scratched laminate counter.

Brett shifted his feet again. "Well, uh. . ."

"It's okay, Brett Robinson. That ain't where I buried the body."

"Oh, I…" He knew he was blushing. "That's not—"

Ruth laughed. "I know what everyone says."

Brett looked uneasy, but when she led the way down the hall, he followed anyway.

The cellar door was stuck in the frame, so she gave it a good tug. "Change of the weather, you know."

"Yeah," Brett said. He held the door open. "Same thing happens at our house."

"These Michigan basements. Tricky in the thaw."

Each step creaked under their weight as they made their way down, the air becoming heavy. The deep freezer hummed from the corner. Hunting clothes and equipment lay neatly stacked and organized along the far wall. She had never thrown away her dead husband's camo jacket and overalls. In fact, she'd had them cuffed and darted, so she could use them herself. Ruth noticed Brett eyeing the hunting rifle mounted above the gear. She chuckled. "We always meant to pour a floor down here, but after a while, I didn't see the point. Besides, ya never know when you might have to hide another body, right?"

"Oh, Mrs. Putnam," Brett said. He shuffled across the dirt floor. He followed her to the back of the cellar, where shelves clung to raw stone walls. "Talking like that is how come people say your husband is buried in the garden."

"My garden! Ha! I wouldn't let that man within fifty feet of my garden."

She patted his arm and turned back to the shelves. She selected a jar of pickles, seasoned with her own dill head. She then chose some pickled beets and two jars of tomatoes. This would help her neighbors make it to their next unemployment check. Brett carefully placed them into his bag, tested its weight.

"That's real nice of you, Mrs. Putnam."

"It's no trouble." She turned to lead the way back upstairs. "We have to look out for one another." On their way through the kitchen, she gestured at the bread on the counter. "Tell your mom thanks for me."

"Will do," Brett said. He opened the screen door. "Take care."

It slammed shut.

*

Robert had kicked open that same screen door ten years ago and yanked Ruth behind him, tearing the sleeve of her Easter dress. He forced her down the porch steps as she stumbled and fell, but he kept going, dragging her across the grass and through the mud. She realized he intended to lock her in the Port-O-Potty. Something wild stirred deep inside her and came raging to the surface.

Howling, she brought her legs around and she kicked at her husband's shins. He stopped, turned to confront her. He clamped his other hand around her free arm and shook her.

Ruth threw her foot into his groin, and he doubled over. She raced to her feet and shoved him as hard as she could. Robert toppled backwards and hit the ground. A jagged chunk of metal, debris from their septic work, caught the back of his neck. His head lolled at an unnatural angle.

She dropped to her knees, numb. She blinked at her husband's body. She next became aware of a throbbing inside her shoulder, likely dislocated. She raised her arm, pulling her elbow away. With a violent yank, she forced her upper arm bone back into its socket. Blinding pain shot through her body, and the world dimmed, fringed with stars. Breathing hard, she rose and made her way to the shed. She pulled out a hoe and a shovel, then returned to Robert.

He'd done her the favor of falling near the pit. Wouldn't have to drag him too far. Taking him by the feet, Ruth pulled her husband to the side of the hole. Then, armed with her tools, she slid down and tested the bottom. The clay was hard; she'd need the hoe first. Ruth began whacking at the ground. As splinters of earth cracked loose, she shoveled them out. Her shoulder throbbed, but she kept digging anyway, pushing agony aside.

With the very last of her strength, she pushed Robert until he flopped over the edge and into the pit. She gazed down at him, wondering if she should rearrange him from the haphazard position he'd fallen in, arms and neck twisted like a roadkill deer—but the night sky was lifting. There wasn't enough time.

She filled in the hole, packing the dirt down as she went. And, as the birds were singing began to sing, her task was complete. Just needed Robert's buddies to drop in the new septic tank and that would be it. No one would find him under a 12,000 pound vat of shit.

Dirt caked her ruined Easter dress. She dragged herself to the kitchen and filled a bag with ice. Unfastening the top buttons of her dress, she shrugged it off and let it tumble to the kitchen floor. Ruth leaned against the sink and placed the cold pack on her bare skin. The ice hurt, but the hurt felt good. Everything, she realized, felt good. From the broken blisters on her palms to the spasms in her back. She took in a slow breath. Things were going to be different.

THE EMPTY CHAIR

STUART GINSBERG

The mattresses' empty indentation flares
downward.
The cold crevice
of a once warm partner
retiring to the other side of the bed,
imagining what it was like holding her head.

An empty chair taunting,
the survivor longing,
she talks to him by the light of the candle.
They imagine their child by the mantle
sticking the log in the fire.
How she used to sing in the choir.

An empty chair stares
in stasis,
unique traits disappearing.
The limbo of living,
a vegetative state never recovered,
afflicted with torment.
What the chair meant
to them,
they know
as others soon will too.

STILL LIFE

CAROLL SUN YANG

We met in a country club break room, each with eighteen years behind us. Two late-blooming summer virgins fated to sit across from one another at a lopsided banquet table, rich men's day-old meats and *brûlée* spread before us. Fellow employees flanked us with their world-weary bodies and gossip, each a touch jaded in their own way, showing delicate trails of wrinkles on hard worn skin made prominent under the cheap fluorescent lighting. Charming, salt-and-pepper-haired career bartenders flirted with spray-tanned banquet ladies sporting French-manicured nails. We did not realize then that they were once like us. How could we yet? I was barely nubile, a hard green plum. You were hardly virile, fumbling paws still too big for you.

I was suffocating in a female cummerbund, starched whites and slippery black heels. You were outfitted in a Grecian white caddy uniform, lowered visor and a Marlboro tucked coolly behind your ear. Your eyes took all of me in, stricken electric-blue under the flickering lights. My eyes felt like bedroom braves and played fresh games with you. We were flushing, sun-kissed creatures emitting that variety of young bright light that we will only ever be blessed with on rare occasions.

I bit my bottom lip. Chewed on my straw. Tried to memorize your face with every glance. Your pupils dilated, just as the teen magazines said they would—you really liked me. Your mouth curled itself into an outrageous grin, your cleft "winked," and I felt sick. I told you I was failing in algebra. You lit up and said you liked math. All of the other chatter in the room became muffled, sounds receding and pitching forward as if we were drifting off to sleep. A warning hum was born in me and a deal was sealed.

*

You said you could help me with the math but only if I would teach you to dance. We locked ourselves in my forever humid bedroom, shut the cheap burgundy drapes, let our cumbersome uniforms fall to the stained shag, piece by piece we teased, okay don't look! In oversized pajama shirts advertising athletic shoes and fresh hamburgers, we danced on the bed. (When I see us now, I love us then). We ate Doritos and nursed warm beers. We worried about nothing. Our eyes locked and retreated as we drew scented-marker drawings of a hallucinatory nature on each other's skin, diamond-eyed cobalt snakes and colorful exit-less mazes. We settled on our bellies, chewing pencils and trying to solve some difficult equation, but stopped when you kissed me real. I had not known a tongue other than mine.

*

That summer was the longest one I had ever felt, bearing a strand of magical nights that ended in a sun that always rose too soon. After midnight we would sneak away from the others to cruise in your mocha-flavored Oldsmobile, chain-smoking as we glided and creaked over moonlit asphalt. I never smoked until you.

Inhaling the fertile rows of farmland mingling with vanilla-scented car freshener—God, the sweet stench of it all. The Santa Ana wind nipping at our fingers as we made easy wavelike motions out the windows. We tuned into staticky classic rock stations and sang out of sync together.

We always parked at the same spot near the sea. We let our backs lean against the base of a great sandy slope, side-by-side we were mesmerized by the phosphorescence breaking. We christened them stony lightning ghosts and believed we owned them. We tried to spill poems out into the salty air, whispering against the crash of waves while trying to make clumsy virgin love. It was a wondrous season of teasing, near penetrations and encouraging whispers. Sometimes we hid in the lifeguard tower with that dank plaid blanket swaddling us, our vapors separated from the fog of beach by nothing. You were patient and promised to be true. Our first time was so painless that I asked you did we just do it? And you said yes, I think so. One night we dared to lie together on the winding tar of the Pacific Coast Highway, kissing until we could see the glare of a distant car speeding towards us. We ran as fast as we could on our skinny legs, tripping and whooping towards the water and when we got to the black foamy edge, I said that I would die if you died. I think you said, me too.

*

You passed me from friend to friend, let them feel me as my head lolled on its loose stem. I saw my own hands grabbing blue-jeaned thighs and stroking all-o'clock shadows, as if for dear life. The *faux* nails were long, square and cherry red. You had convinced me this looked sexy and felt good on your flesh. I saw locks of my own polished hair, draped on their young laps. So many hard zippers and buttons brushed my cheek. They unbuttoned my shirt. I had no bra. I felt small and firm as they felt me roughly. One of them dared to kiss a nipple and a primal sound escaped me. I still felt the electricity in that. My head throbbed but not with pain, my body felt stuffed with hot cotton. There were angry liquored words about who was next, one of the boys snarled and threw me onto the night cool grass. The dew felt good. You flinched and some of your playing cards fell to the ground. You picked them up and put them in some neat order. Your mute jaw was tight. I thought I saw a thick vein run down your neck and disappear into your shirt. Your lashes were a sorry kind of veil. You sat at that glass table, blank-faced while your friends pounded one another senselessly with their alienating horseplay. You held your cards, looking at them as if they still mattered but no one was playing. I wanted in.

My sleeveless bluebell blouse was flung over the garden hose and the once clean silk skirt trampled. I still wore my pink panties, the ones with the crimson rose motif. I was beyond feeling naked then, past that kind of inherited shame, as there were more urgent things to confront. I was crying softly into the ground, just within your reach, and my heart was fucking begging at your feet. Did you feel it? Down in the soil, it smelled like rain. The crickets were deafening. I could taste a fuzzy citrus on my tongue. Smell the pungent perfume of overripe flora, a cheap smell. My hand fondled the glittering pebbles of a manicured landscape. I felt clover pushing through. The sky was clear, and the divine stars still twinkled, it seemed outrageous. I even whispered in a choked voice that I hoped you would hear, fuck you stars. My favorite tortoise shell barrette was trapped under your heel. I never did see it again, or find one like it, believe me I have looked.

Your friends went indoors when they grew bored of the backyard game, but you stayed, sitting alone at a table littered with junk food wrappers, playing cards, drink sticky glasses, ash, and boyish trinkets. You smoked with long draws that made you sigh on exhale. You were swigging huge gulps of beer and wiping your lips on your bare arm. I could see the yellow light of tall streetlamps and the heavens shining off of the trail you left. Your hands that handled me all through the summer, were now shuffling a dead hand. I knew you were looking at me. You thought I was asleep, but I was not, I was waiting. I had nowhere better to go. This was someone else's home sweet home, but it was mine that night too. We stayed that way for hours, listening to the loop of our favorite Led Zeppelin album trilling through an open window. When that song "Tangerine" started playing, I felt it so much. I prayed you did too. It was too beautiful.

The music never stops. It is patient and promises to be true. It teases and the penetration is bit by bit. It is painful sometimes. Youthful transgressions bleed through a special sieve. Flecks of shimmering gold appear. The ocean continues glowing without us. The Indian summers are always on time. Lemonade and moonshine are forever. There are many new queens being born. Spades too. A first is never not that. The last is absolute. You hold a dead hand. I am still a midnight nude, dewy blades of grass bending under the weight of my plea. You are still sitting there waiting to be a man.

CONTRIBUTORS

JANET BOHAC's stories have appeared in numerous anthologies and literary magazines. Her travel and food writing appeared in *Caribbean Travel & Life*. She is the author of *Evidence Of The Outer World*, a collection of short fiction. She was writer-in-residence at Austin Peay State University and taught screenwriting at University of Miami and Florida International University. She was a screenwriting fellow at The American Film Institute.

HOLLY CARIGNAN has an old, unused MA in Psychology and, more recently, a BS in Biochemistry. When she is not slogging away in a hospital lab, she is home writing by computer light in the comfortable darkness of her messy house. Holly lives in Connecticut with her three irresistible, pesty, entertaining cats.

DANIEL DAMIANO is an award-winning playwright, award-nominated actor, screenwriter, poet, and novelist based in Brooklyn, NY. His plays have been produced throughout many areas of the U.S. as well as London, England and Sydney & Melbourne, Australia. His acclaimed play *Day of the Dog* was published by Broadway Play Publishing. His acclaimed debut novel, *The Woman in the Sun Hat*, was published in March 2021 by Fandango 4 Art House. Website: www.danieldamiano.com

SIDNEY J. DRAGON was born in New Orleans but has spent his adult life in Central Florida. He's a writer and actor who enjoys spending time in his kitchen preparing traditional (and not so traditional) Cajun/Creole based meals. His first novel, *Cities of the Dead: Sally's Sorrow*, has slipped into the world of out of print, but he hopes to revive it. His second novel, *The Chantry*, is in its final rewrite stages. His household consists of his wife Amy, their son Phoenix, daughter Ember, adopted brother Bear, dog Dixiebelle, and cat Hemmingway,

The daughter of Russian immigrants, **GLADYS DUBOVSKY**, now 105 years-old, survived her abusive childhood by finding refuge in poetry. In the winter of 1940, when she was 25, she took a poetry class taught by W.H. Auden at the New School in Manhattan. She met with him privately to discuss her poetry and found that his encouragement forever changed her. Her time with Auden is accounted in the book *W.H. Auden, Poetry, and Me: A 102-Year-Old Reluctant Poet Reflects on Life, Poetry, and Her Famous Teacher*. Gladys lives in Midtown Manhattan.

KELLY JEAN FITZSIMMONS is a writer, educator, and storyteller who lives in Astoria, Queens. Her nonfiction work has appeared in *Human Parts, Marie Claire*, and *Hippocampus Magazine*, among others. Her most recent play, a superhero comedy, *All I Want Is One More Meanwhile*, made its Midwest premiere at Otherworld Theatre in Chicago. Combining her love for narrative nonfiction and theater, Kelly Jean created *No, YOU Tell It!*, a storytelling series dedicated to performing true-life tales with a twist. Learn more and listen to the podcast at noyoutellit.com.

VICKI HENDRICKS is the author of noir novels *Miami Purity, Iguana Love, Voluntary Madness, Sky Blues*, and *Cruel Poetry*, an Edgar Award Finalist in 2008. Her short stories are mostly collected in *Florida Gothic Stories*. She currently lives in central Florida, the rural locale of her most recent novel *Fur People*.

JACK McCLELAND is an award-winning playwright raised in New England where he draws on many of his stories. His play *The Good Life* was the winner of the Summer Solstices Theatre Award and was produced by both the Quaigh Theater and The Image Theater in New York City His play *Hardball* was a 2016 finalist for the Heideman Award at the Actor's Theatre of Louisville. His plays have been produced in New York City and around the country. He lives in New

York City with his wife Elizabeth Campbell and their multi-talented cats. He is a member of the Dramatists Guild.

JIM MOSS is a videographer and playwright who dabbles in short stories. His plays have been produced off-Broadway in New York, and at theatres in numerous cities, including London, Los Angeles, Chicago, Miami, Orlando, Tampa, and Denver. In 2018 his play *Tagged* won three awards: First place in Theatre Odyssey's One-Act Play Festival in Sarasota, Best Lab Works Production at the Pittsburgh New Works Festival, and the British Theatre Challenge in London. His science fiction short story "Still Life With Grave Juice" can be found in the *Diabolical Plots Year Four Anthology*.

LEONARD NASH received a Florida Book Award for *You Can't Get There from Here and Other Stories* (Kitsune Books, 2007). His work has appeared in the *South Dakota Review, The Seattle Review, Fort Lauderdale Magazine,* the *South Florida Sun-Sentinel, Gulf Stream Magazine,* and in several anthologies including *15 Views of Miami* (Burrow Press, 2014), and *Flash! Writing the Very Short Story* (Norton, 2018). He has taught creative writing workshops at Florida International University, Miami Dade College, the Sanibel Island Writers Conference, the Rosemary Beach Writers Conference, and elsewhere. He lives in Hollywood, Florida.

JESSICA OESTERLE is a two-time first prize winner of the An Beal Bocht Flash Fiction Contest and a recipient of the 2019 First Quarter Honorable Mention from the Galaxy Press Writers of the Future Contest. Her fiction and poetry have appeared in various small presses, including recent online publication in *The Wild Word* and *Please See Me*. Originally from a working farm in mid-Michigan, Jessica is an MFA student in the CCNY Creative Writing Program and a full-time commercial furniture designer in New York City. She shares a pre-war Bronx apartment with her husband Bill and their rescue pitbull Fiona.

RORY PENLAND has written skits, short stories, screenplays, and novels. He is also an established stand-up comedian, accomplished actor, professional singer, and artist. In 2002, Penland's screenplay *Deadly Species* was produced and distributed by Artisan Films. While living in China, he worked on the Disney animated show *Super Robot Monkey Team Hyper Force Go!* as well as Canada's *Biker Mice From Mars*. Penland is currently writing stories for *The Tales of The Vampyr* and *Post-Apocalyptic Bachelor's Guides* series of books, published by Palm Circle Press.

DEBBIE SHANNON has an MFA in creative writing from Florida International University. She is the author of three books: *The Fisherman, A Crowded Loneliness: The story of loss, survival, and resilience of a Peter Pan Child of Cuba*, and *W.H. Auden, Poetry, and Me: A 102-year-old reluctant poet reflects on life, poetry, and her famous teacher*. She lives in upstate New York. When she's not writing, Debbie spends most of her time reading, cooking, and traveling the world in search of the perfect fish taco. Visit her online at https://debbieshannon.com/

CAROLL SUN YANG earned her BFA at Art Center College of Design, an MFA in Creative Writing from Antioch University and holds certification as a Psychosocial Rehabilitation Specialist. Her work appears in *Hunger Mountain, The Los Angeles Review of Books, Columbia Journal, Diagram, Juked, Barrelhouse,* and her piece "The Waist That You Are From" was a Pushcart nominee. She identifies as a Korean-American writer/artist/career-waitress/vintage peddler/mother/wife breathing in Los Angeles, Ca. She is at work on a mixed-genre collection titled "Guest Check." www.carollsunyang.com, IG: franzialux_rellickroad

Comments? Questions? Found errors?

Please, reach out to us!

info@palmcirclepress.net

Sign up for our mailing list at **palmcirclepress.net**

LEAVE A REVIEW

I would be extremely grateful if you could take just a minute to write a review on Amazon about this book. Even if the review is brief (2 or 3 sentences) that would be incredibly helpful. Recommending this book to a friend doesn't hurt either!

Thank you and I love you!!!

Please visit Amazon to leave a review.

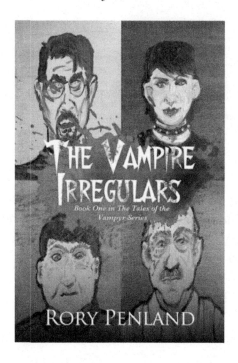

DARK LORDS OF THE TRAILER PARK

Short Stories
Lee Anderson

Beautiful losers, smooth criminals, deranged lovers…

…driven by an unblinking vision of a morally depleted world.
The characters in these stories are charged by a bruised grace,
enabling them to find redemption in the most unlikely of places.

To Learn More, Visit Amazon Today!

THE MOST BEAUTIFUL INSANITY

South Beach Crime Thriller Series, Book One
Heather Wilde

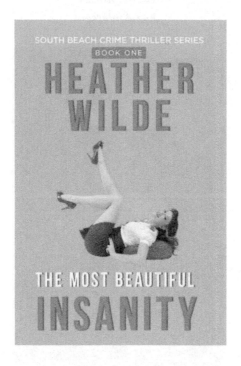

Beauty can be a burden...

From decadent parties to luxurious nightclubs, this is a thrilling and often frightening incursion into the hearts and minds of modern-day fashionistas. Model Ophelia Lake has an addiction--to Drexel Waters, a suave, sociopathic male model. When Drexel inadvertently causes the overdose death of a younger wannabe, her billionaire father becomes hell-bent on revenge.

To Learn More, Visit Amazon Today!

SWEET DEMON LOVE BABY

South Beach Crime Thriller Series, Book Two
Heather Wilde

Nobody really knows who anybody else is...

Trace Strickland is a homicide detective whose controversial career hangs in the balance. When his fiancé turns up dead from a knife wound in her South Beach apartment, he becomes the first suspect. Investigating her death to clear his name, he discovers her prior involvement in an underworld of violence, sex trafficking, and other illicit dealings he never suspected.

To Learn More, Visit Amazon Today!

WHAT HAPPENED AT SISTERS CREEK

A Horror Novel
Lee Anderson

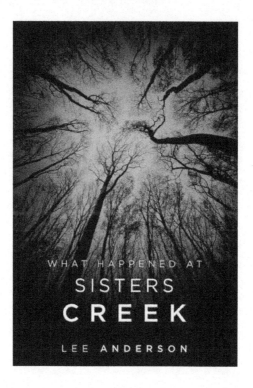

There are places in the woods you should never go...

Charlie Sparks is the sheriff of a small town, his career derailed by rampant scandal and corruption. When faced with solving the gruesome campsite murder of a young family, Sparks suspects two recent escape convicts. The sheriff and his search party set out into the woods to find them but instead discover an unthinkable horror, driven by a voracious hunger for human flesh.

To Learn More, Visit Amazon Today!

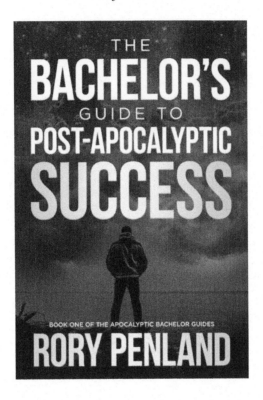

Made in the USA
Monee, IL
18 May 2021